Drink Up, Darling

HARVEY OLIVER BAXTER

Paperback ISBN: 978-1-7395208-9-2

Ebook ISBN: 978-1-7395208-8-5

Cover illustration by Ashe Arends (@spookgeist on Instagram)

Praise for Drink Up, Darling

Drink Up, Darling is a beautiful story about the power of love, second chances and friendship. When you're at your lowest, all you need is someone to see you, flaws and all. To remind you just how human you can be.

— SYD NEBEN, AUTHOR OF *ANTIQUE ROMAN*

A dark and sensuous story of love—platonic, romantic, and everything in between—and acceptance, *Drink Up, Darling* is another fantastic addition to Baxter's impressive vampiric collection, this one reminding us that the love we share with one another is based in acceptance, and knowing that every single last bit of us, flaws and all, will be accepted and cherished by another (or more, wink wink).

— SHEPARD DISTASIO, AUTHOR OF *VEIL US IN GOLD*

Stunning. Delicious. Devastatingly divine. I'm obsessed with *Drink Up, Darling* and its positively queer vampires!

— BEN ALDERSON, AUTHOR OF *THE HAUNTING OF WILLIAM THORN*

Drink Up, Darling is decadently gothic, an ode to the classic vampire story, with as much sweetness as it has bite.

— JADE CHURCH, AUTHOR OF *GET EVEN*

Drink Up, Darling is a lush, tantalizing treat that turns a well-known vampire trope on its head in a satisfying and delightful way. Fans of AMC's Interview with the Vampire will eat this up and leave no crumbs.

— MARS ADLER, AUTHOR OF *FIRST CREATION*

Drink Up, Darling

To the LGBTQ+ community
Past, present, and future

Author Note

This book contains some topics and themes I believe should be addressed before you begin:

- References to suicide/suicidal intent
- Death of a family member/friend (mentioned as past events)
- Homophobia/transphobia (referenced as past experiences)
- PTSD manifesting as shadows
- References to alcoholism
- References to the AIDS pandemic
- Mentions of domestic abuse (past events, non-sexual)
- Murder
- Blood drinking
- Consensual sexual content
- Mild dissociation

Chapter One

Five days after his intended untimely death, Dariel stepped out of his apartment complex to be met with the tears of God.

He thanked the doorman, swiftly stepping out with one hand gripping his faux-feather coat tight to his chest, the other firmly gripped to his black case. He almost marched straight into the storm, but abruptly stopped at the top of the stone steps, still hidden under the canopy of the building, and rolled his eyes at the scene before him. With a sigh and shoulders slouching, he weighed his options.

It could have at least tried to snow, he thought.

Three women strode past using their cropped leather jackets to form tents over their heads, muttering merry squeals between each other as their flared, low-rise jeans soaked up the stream from an overflowing drain. One of them wore novelty 2007 glasses, another had tinsel in place of a belt. Dariel hadn't slept a wink the last few days; people up at all hours, bashing around neighbouring apartments and floors. Apparently New Year's Eve isn't enough. Or maybe he was getting old. He didn't really have the patience for things like that anymore. There would have been a time where he'd party for days on end, forgetting himself in music and booze, but not anymore. Not now.

The dams of the earth literally bursting from above that very moment didn't help his mood. He'd just done his makeup and blow dried his hair. The first time he'd made an effort since his agent dropped him last month.

A taxi pulled up a moment later, sludging up to the curb and covering the reflection of rippling red and green lights in the puddle over the drain, cutting Dariel's thoughts short. With a deeper sigh, he threw his bag over his hair, and hurried out into the rain, slipping into the back of the cab.

He wasn't miserable, you must understand. This just wasn't how he'd planned to start this new year.

He was meant to die.

Well, sort of.

Plans changed.

"Where to, mate?"

The soul currently going by the name Dariel Hale had lived many lives. Some he loved, others he'd much rather forget, but 'Dariel' had been his longest stint, and he was sad it had to come to an end. He had it all planned out, and had financed for months. The media would devour it; his face plastered over the front of newspapers with his name mentioned on radio stations. He was somewhat of a celebrity in the fashion world, you see; finding his niche and shooting to fame in the late nineties. Dariel Hale jackets were all the rage, you'd see them everywhere. But like everything, he had an expiry date. Agencies eventually grew tired of him, his designs no longer kept with the times—he was no longer relevant. So in keeping with the demise of his career, the media would get over his death, and everyone would move on. Probably very quickly. You might find some of his jackets listed on second hand sites. *Rare! Unworn! Hanging in the back of my wardrobe for years!* Even then though, he doubted the general public would care.

He would have long left London before he could measure how valued he really was in the designer scene though—having already settled into life number five by then. He'd thought about changing his age this time; beginning at twenty no longer seemed old enough. His face might not show his age, but he sure felt it. He considered trying out his actual age, which was twenty-four. Give or take forty years.

Twenty-four would work. It would be ambiguous enough to allow at least fifteen years before people would start questioning his moisturising routine. Then he could gauge the adequate age to kill himself again. Or he might just disappear. He'll decide when the time comes.

For now, his plans had been put on hold though. Dariel Hale's body was meant to be discovered in his bathtub nearly a week ago. That damn email really threw a spanner in the works.

Who sends emails on New Year's Eve anyway? Isn't that an internationally recognised day of not *sending emails?* He'd thought as he sat at his desk in his frustratingly empty apartment, chewing on his nails in the shadows; the glow of the laptop screen burning his retinas. He'd had to downsize his apartment recently because no one had hired him in months, and his money had quickly dwindled. Keeping up appearances is far too expensive, and he'd always had expensive tastes, even in his previous lives. He never bothered unpacking the boxes in his new flat, since they'd all have to get packed away again once the place went back on the market. No point in further inconveniencing the strangers who'd have to distribute all his belongings after his death since he had no living relatives on record. He didn't bother writing a will, there really was no point. He was in the process of writing out a note to his lovely cleaner, Sheila, and organising the concoction of drugs he'd stashed up for that evening, when the email popped up. He could have ignored it, gone ahead with his plan: getting his silk pyjamas on, climbing into his bathtub with a Talisker in one hand, the prop pills in the sink beside him, and forcing himself to vomit. It was the evening of the last day of the year, so they wouldn't have found his body until at earliest the following afternoon, or maybe even later, depending on how many people noticed he'd not been down for his daily newspaper. Regardless of how long it took, they'd find him, make an easy conclusion from the scene, realise his heart was no longer beating, and after failed resuscitation attempts, he'd be pronounced dead at the scene. Such a tragedy.

He hadn't quite worked out the logistics of escaping the morgue, but he was sure he'd manage it. He didn't even need his eyes open to use his manipulation on humans around him, and he'd used his abilities on enough people in his many lives to know it would all go swimmingly. Perks of being the inhuman man he was.

Maybe the defibrillator would restart his heart after forty years, he had wondered if that was a possibility, but he brushed it off. It was highly unlikely. Nothing else had.

Anyway, this plan was all for nothing, because as it happened, Dariel Hale decided to open this email, and the following Friday, he was in the back of a taxi, lighting up a cigarette on his way to a grand manor house two hours away, preparing to meet a man he would become the personal designer for. A month-long job; his first for a long while.

Maybe rebirth could wait.

"You off to a party?" The driver made sure to take a good head to foot gaze at Dariel's ensemble. It was clear he didn't recognise him, which was a good thing, but the prolonged, strained-neck stare was —Dariel quickly decided—highly unnecessary. Surely the home-made feathered jacket and midnight-sparkled eyeshadow was not the most extravagant thing he'd seen in the back of his cab over the holidays. *Surely.*

"Just a meal," Dariel deadpanned as the taxi pulled away into the night, splashing a poor bloke walking past on the pavement. Dariel adjusted himself in the back seat, sliding his case to the space beside him as rows of streetlights bleared through the window in pulses. Maybe he had one too many layers on, shame none of them were waterproof. Hopefully by the time they arrived at the destination, an entirely new season will have emerged. The duality of British weather.

"Looking very dolled up, mate. You one of those, erm, *performers?*"

Oh great, he's a talker. Dariel held his tongue and smiled into the wing mirror. *Let the bloke fluster and try to figure it out.*

"Listen, not like I got a problem. You do what you want, you know. I got a mate who erm... he, she, it, no... you know, dresses up and..." The driver waved his hand to finish the sentence.

Okay, I don't have the energy for this. Dariel tilted his head to rest against the window, the condensation cold against his skin. "I'm just a man who likes his fashion." He said it matter-of-factly, with the hope it would put the conversation to bed.

It did. For a long time.

They drove through the city for over an hour, Dariel allowing himself to observe everything going on that evening. At some point he asked the driver whether he minded if he had another cigarette, and the driver responded with a simple "sure." Dariel wound down the window a little to let the smoke out this time, tipping his head back against the seat and closing his eyes as the smoke swam into his lungs. The sounds of life swirled around him from outside as the rain grew lighter and the night grew on.

He wound the window back up as they reached the outskirts of the city and the lights dimmed, inviting the silence, and letting himself dwell on everything that led up to this point.

With his eyes tightly closed, Dariel dreamed. He dreamed of his first life—always the place his thoughts wandered to before anything else. He dreamed of Annette, his beautiful wife, and of the cottage they owned in a quiet village up north in the early sixties. He dreamed of the birds tweeting every morning as he lifted the sash window they always had to keep propped open with a stone from the garden. He dreamed of the flowers that grew there and the evenings they sat out in odd chairs, looking up at the stars. Annette always smiled in his dreams, the biggest, brightest beam across her freckled face. She'd make jokes sometimes, and in others she'd be baking something or occasionally hanging out washing. His favourite dreams were when they were walking along the canal together, or when they'd take a picnic up to the fields where Annette's parents lived. They married young, as you did in those days, but he knew she was everything and more to him, and he wished for an eternity with her.

Then, because no one stopped him, his dreams would wander to that day in the kitchen, the morning sun painting the walls yellow as Annette, dressed in her denim pinafore, a peach head-band keeping her hair back with daisy earrings hanging from each earlobe, reached down to hold her belly *that way*.

Dariel's head flicked up and their eyes locked, her smile beaming again.

"Our baby?" He always asked in disbelief.

"Our little Sparrow."

Then the next memory *always* came. Straight away, no warn-ing, no transition.

Just flames.

"You asleep there, mate?"

Dariel startled awake with a sharp jolt, the seatbelt jamming into his throat as his eyes burst open in a panic.

He looked down to his hands before processing anything else, the shadows crawling all over his skin, enveloping his whole body like mist. His dim reflection always showed them, smothering his wide eyes, and then, as always, the fear that everyone else around him could also see them would hit.

He knew that wasn't true, though.

No one else could ever see them.

Without further thought, Dariel reached into his coat pocket and produced a hip flask, unscrewing the cap before the driver even had time to notice. He took one quick swig of blood, shaking his head. If the driver saw, he didn't say anything. It looked completely normal, just a guy taking a quick sip of his favourite whisky, nothing more.

He watched the road for a while; head back on the glass, eyes forced open in focus. If he looked at the trees and telephone wires and the distant, blinking city lights, making up scenarios in his head or thinking about plans, then he could keep the dreams at bay.

He didn't want to forget them.

He'd just never been good at managing them.

Once they turned off the main roads and began to trail down more country lanes, Dariel decided to pull out his laptop. A pit had begun to form in his stomach—not from hunger, from worry. It came out of nowhere, he'd tried really hard to keep all negative thoughts at bay, but the closer and closer they got to the destination, Dariel's nerves intensified.

He'd saved the email as a document to access any time, just in case.

He let his eyes scan over every word; second guessing the time, the plan, his decision. He wanted to make sure he'd read it all correctly—despite having gone over it a dozen times.

Dear Mr Dariel Hale,

Apologies for my lack of professionalism, I will admit I'm not well versed in hiring designers, so forgive me if this is not the way to go about contacting you, but I could not find any other means of getting in touch. I thought I would try my luck first.
My name is Godwin Peters, I'm the sole owner of Grandshaw

Manor just north of Abingdon, and I have recently decided it is time to update my clothes.

I'm a man of middle age, and have spent quite a long time wearing the same dreary outfits day in, day out. I stumbled across your work years ago in a magazine inside my newspaper, and it would be a great dream of mine if you would do me the pleasure of helping me redesign my wardrobe.

Of course, I expect to pay you as I understand this will take quite some time. I'm presuming this would be something you could mostly do from the comfort of your own studio once you have all the necessary information, but we can discuss accommodation if necessary. I have £200,000 to offer, though a higher price can be negotiated as I am not sure of your rates! Please do not take this offer as an insult, I am a huge admirer of your work.

If you accept this offer, I would love to invite you to my home for dinner on 5th January at 7pm so we can become acquainted and discuss further.

If this is not the best way to contact you but you are still interested, would you be able to let me know the contact details of perhaps your agent or assistant who handles your business enquiries?

Kind regards,
Mr Godwin Peters

His address was listed at the bottom, but Dariel had already made up his mind before he'd even seen the payment offer. He enjoyed the manner in which this gentleman wrote, causing a grin to form on Dariel's face. Reading it again in the taxi only reminded him of why he was so quick to accept in the first place.

He was doing the right thing.

Plus, the money was a huge bonus. He'd not seen figures like that for ages.

. . .

"You a businessman of some sort then?" The driver finally piped up after another prolonged silence. Not a single car had passed them in a while, and it was clear they were getting close, even if Dariel could only see the silhouette of trees shielding the moonlight. He had no real idea where they were going, but thought it shouldn't be too much further.

"Something like that," Dariel responded absently, wishing if the man really wanted to talk, that he stopped sounding so quizzical all of the time. Like he was trying to figure Dariel out. It made him uncomfortable.

"Hmm. Interesting. Forgive me for prying, you can't blame me for being a little curious. A pretty boy like you getting all glammed up for a two-hour journey to a posh house in the middle of nowhere. It's not a journey I've done before, let's just say."

Dariel inwardly sighed. Instead of responding, he lit up another cigarette, his fingers shaking slightly.

The driver gave up after a few huffs and puffs, tapping his fingers on the steering wheel in a passive aggressive manner.

After an eternity of winding paths and gravel roads, branches and weeds slapping the bonnet and scraping the side of the doors, the taxi reached a gate, one too ornate to be anything younger than Victorian made. The pointed arrow heads shot up towards the sky, illuminated by nothing but a singular 19th century streetlamp buried half amongst the oak and birch.

"This the right place, kid?"

Kid? I'm sixty-four. Dariel was used to the assumption he was young though; he couldn't blame anyone for reaching that conclusion.

Before Dariel could ask to be dropped off there, the gates began to swing open with a squeak, and the driver didn't hesitate before accelerating up the raised gravel path, throwing Dariel back into his seat slightly.

He hadn't been able to see the house yet, he thought he may have caught a glimpse of perhaps a turret sticking out from above the trees, but it wasn't until they turned the final corner when the manor truly came into view.

It was like entering a new world, the arching branches of the drive opening out onto a vast driveway before the house, the trees ending almost suddenly as the view from that height became clear. The house was lit, however only by the front two windows; the rest of the stone manor residing in the shadows of the night.

From this angle and limited lighting, it looked as if the house resided on a cliff face, perched upon a sharp drop into the oblivion of countryside, though Dariel was sure it was not. He knew it would be much more impressive during the day. The true view would have to wait.

Upon replying to Mr Peter's initial email, Dariel was given the offer of staying the night to ensure a relaxed evening. He was of course hesitant at first, but after experiencing how tedious the journey was, he was glad he'd accepted. Even if it all turned out to be a scam, worst case scenario, he'd just have to kill him.

Dariel had heard the taxi driver gasp once the house came into view, but was too focused on processing it himself to make a comment.

"So, I believe this is you then," the driver said, winding down his window and sticking his head out to get a better look at the place.

"Yes, thank you. I appreciate you driving me all the way out here, how much do I owe you?"

"You one of those male escort things?" the driver asked, his head still hanging out of the window. He continued. "You gotta be, surely. Dressed like that, coming out here to some posh bloke's house. How much is he paying you? Is it by the hour?"

"How much do I owe you?" Dariel asked again, agitation in his voice and hand on the door ready to leave.

The driver popped his head back inside and turned to Dariel, a sneer attached to his face. "Isn't it the receiver who normally drives to the prostitute? Or is this the secret location? Is this one of those big orgy things? Look, I'm not gonna tell anyone, I'm just curious, you know?"

He could snap his neck, drink him dry right there if he wanted. Make it quick, or make him suffer. Dariel could have done a lot of things in that moment, but instead, he smiled. "I haven't done that since the eighties," he said, then watched as the driver's face dropped and his brow knitted itself into that of both shock and confusion.

He didn't give him time to process or ask Dariel to repeat what he said. He wanted to let the thought ruminate, so he quickly reached into his pocket for his wallet, produced four crisp twenty-pound notes, threw them in the driver's direction, and exited the vehicle.

"Keep the change," he said, turning his back to the car and heading for the front door without a second glance.

Chapter Two

It may have been a mistake letting the taxi drive off before he'd even knocked on the door, but he wanted nothing more to do with that bloke, and thought he'd rather walk all the way back to central London than endure more questions linking back to the fact he was obviously a queer man. He could have used his manipulation to change the subject, but he'd quite frankly grown tired of it all. It was always the same, he couldn't escape it. He wasn't going to change himself for other people, so he grew to learn how to block it out, or at least try to.

The thought did pass him: what if this Godwin was worse? What if he'd taken the journey to hell, only to be met with the real fire once he arrived. But Godwin had made it clear he was a fan of Dariel's work. It was hard to tell when people were being sincere via email, but he had planned for most outcomes.

There was no going back now.

Dariel stepped up to the giant oak and iron bolted door, and slammed the brass knocker into the wood three times for good measure.

At first there was no answer, then a small light blinked off in the bay window to his left and he heard movement. Footsteps on polished stone.

Godwin had been waiting.

The door creaked open and just as Dariel could make out the grand staircase and red-carpet runner, a figure emerged from behind the wood. Mr Peters himself, surely.

He was dressed in a neat grey suit and was of average height; broad shouldered and round bellied, with greying but still thick waves on his head, woven with golden brown tones to match his equally full and well-maintained beard. It was his eyes Dariel noticed first though, a bright but deep shade of green, hidden behind a round set of tortoise shell glasses. His eyes *smiled*.

"Ahh, Mr Hale! I was worried you'd gotten lost!" Mr Peters beamed, both arms outstretched as if to invite a hug. Dariel awkwardly grinned back, not too intensely, and nodded his head in greeting, both hands gripping his bag.

There was a mild beat of awkwardness as Dariel stared at the warmth and vivid colour of the interior whilst still being stood out in monochrome, but Mr Peters eventually stepped aside and ushered for Dariel to enter.

"Do come in! It's freezing out there, I hope you weren't standing for too long. It was absolutely pouring earlier, awful wind too, glad to see it has died off. Come on, you'll soon warm up!" Mr Peters continued to talk merrily as Dariel stepped over the threshold, and the door was closed behind him with a loud echo.

Mr Peters brushed off the cold from his shoulders as Dariel's gaze wandered to the vast emptiness of the home; hyperaware of the eerie sense of *nothingness* that had quickly creeped up his spine. It was decorated the way you would expect a well-preserved stately home to be, reds and golds of grandeur, however nothing of the design suggested it was lived in and *loved*. No personal touches, no hints of the man before him, just stone walls and too high door frames. It was completely silent save for their shoes on the polished, chequered floor, and Mr Peters' continuous one-sided conversation.

Dariel hadn't intended to be rude, he simply had a habit of absorbing new surroundings before introducing himself.

"Let me take your bag, I'm sure you've been travelling for a while, it's time you relaxed and made yourself at home."

"Thank you," Dariel said, handing his case to Mr Peters and watching as he simply placed it to his side. Dariel presumed a butler or maid would perhaps take it up to his room. He hadn't sensed anyone else in the building, no more heartbeats or breaths, but it was a large house, perhaps they were just too far away.

"Let me take that gorgeous coat too, this house gets surprisingly warm. Stunning, by the way. It's a beauty. One of your own?" He seemed almost excited. In awe.

Dariel nearly snapped his client's hand away in shock, but he remembered he'd hidden the flask at the bottom of his locked case, so the jacket was hiding no secrets. He let Mr Peters slide the feather jacket and under coat off, noting how careful and delicate his hands were as he shrugged them off his shoulders. They were quiet for a moment, his client's warm hand briefly making contact with his bare neck, making him shudder. It stunned him, the detailed brush of hands over his body, heat rising to his cheeks. Then just as quickly as the moment arose, it passed, and Dariel's coats were now in the hands of his client, who folded them over one arm and told him he would hang them in the room down the hall.

Dariel finally processed the question. "Oh, sorry, yes. It's mine, I designed it." He breathed out heavily and shook his head to remain in the present.

Mr Peters beamed, stroking a keen hand over the fabric. "Oh, marvellous. I thought it might be." He directed Dariel towards the east wing of the house and began to explain a bit about the rooms ahead.

Dariel allowed himself to be led down the corridor, taking in every detail of the building surrounding him: the maroon wallpaper up to shoulder height with a cream trim, the bare stone wall rising to the ceiling beneath it, and the extravagant picture frames lining the walls with paintings of people Dariel did not recognise.

"I don't get many visitors, as you can probably tell," Mr Peters said as he led Dariel down to one of the many south facing rooms.

"You have a beautiful home," Dariel said in response. "It's a shame it is not visited more often."

There was nothing about this man that indicated hostility, so Dariel allowed himself to slip into the comfort of the way he normally spoke. "Apologies for my tardiness, you have a lot of winding paths, as I'm sure you're aware."

Mr Peters laughed from his chest. "Oh, tell me about it, gardening is a nightmare." He opened a door leading into a library room with walls lined from floor to ceiling in dark wood shelves, with a giant stained-glass window overlooking the blackness of night on the wall to the left. A large reading lamp in the corner was the only other brightness in the room, along with the roaring grand fire surrounded by marble and a mantlepiece holding a brass clock, but it provided enough ambience to make the room inviting. Two chesterfields were positioned over a Persian rug in the middle of the room, a low table between them, making the fireplace the feature of the room.

"I'm sure you pay your gardeners handsomely." Dariel continued the conversation, hoping maybe it would lead to an explanation on the staffing situation in this place. It did not.

"Oh, indeed! I cannot be trusted with anything sharper than a butter knife—it's terrible honestly. Highly embarrassing." Mr Peters cleared his throat. "Please, make yourself at home. Would you like anything to drink? Tea, coffee, something alcoholic? I have quite the variety of beverages available."

Dariel stepped into the room fully and walked around to one of the chairs, awaiting approval to sit before setting himself onto the soft leather. "Honestly just some tap water will do me right now, if you don't mind." He hated being awkward.

"Of course, sir. Coming right up."

Dariel stopped him before he left the room. "Please, no 'sir'. I am just a man. Dariel is fine."

Mr Peters nodded in the doorway, taking in a deep breath. "Dariel, then. And please, call me Godwin." Another bright smile followed.

Dariel invited the silence as he awaited Godwin's return, letting himself sink into the Chesterfield, tipping his head back with a sigh. He scanned the bookshelves for anything he might have recognised; he was never a big reader, but would occasionally pick up some recommended works. Nothing stood out though, just the dizzying height of the ceiling.

The fire crackled as a log broke and Dariel jolted upright to stare into the blaze. A faint scent of cinnamon graced his nose momentarily and he wiped it away with an itch. The amber glow of the fire seemed to brighten the more he stared at it, entrancing him entirely.

John! Please! Help!

He shook his head abruptly to scare off the thoughts, black shadows curling over his shoulders again. *Not now* he thought as footsteps approached.

The door creaked open fully, and in came Godwin with a tray holding a glass of water, a teapot, and two mugs.

"Here we go. Hope you don't mind but I'm in the mood for a herbal tea, you may have some if you want!" Godwin placed the tray down, popping Dariel's glass on a placemat in front of him, then sat himself opposite Dariel with a relaxed sigh, adjusting his waistcoat as he did so.

Dariel went straight in for a sip of water as if it would calm his nerves. He wasn't *afraid,* he was just not very good at meeting new people—still wasn't, after all these years. Maybe it was a trust thing, that had to be something to do with it.

The fire spat again as Godwin began to speak. "So, Dariel, I thank you for coming again, it truly is an honour."

"Oh, the pleasure is mine, honestly. You were extremely generous with your offer."

Godwin chuckled slightly, his eyes smiling again. "Oh, honestly, I value your work, my friend. I worried it would insult!"

My friend. Very confident, this man, isn't he?

Dariel sucked in his lips. "So, would you prefer to discuss your ideas now or after dinner? I've got some samples and notes in my bag if—"

"After dinner." Godwin cut him off. "If that's okay," he added, tone softening.

"Oh, of course." Dariel sunk into himself again.

Godwin poured himself his first drink and Dariel took close note at how precise he was. A napkin to catch the drips and to dry the tip of the pot. No marks, no mess, all very clean. *I like that,* Dariel thought to himself, smiling inwardly as Godwin continued.

"I'd rather we learn more about each other before we get onto the work! I want you to feel comfortable with me before we begin. Then we can discuss the best way for payment, the visiting schedule and whatnot."

There was something about the way he said it that made Dariel's stomach flutter. He had an attractive voice—low and almost husky sounding, mildly posh but not overbearing. Dariel *had* noticed this straight away, but only now did it sit with him. Godwin was a very... pleasant man.

Don't start being inappropriate, Dariel. You know how you get when you grow too comfortable.

Dariel blushed, brushing away the thoughts as quickly as he could. "Yes, that would be nice. After all, I need to study your personality to really find you a wardrobe to match."

Study your personality? Seriously, Dariel. Tone it down a bit.

It didn't seem to faze Godwin though, in fact, it made him grin ever so slightly wider, brow raising. "Excellent!" He beamed. "Well then! No harm in a little introduction before we eat, I suppose. Tell me, what got you into fashion design?"

Dariel deflated at this, having been asked this too many times before, but he didn't want to come across unprofessional—after all, this was the first time Godwin himself had asked this. It was just the ninetieth time Dariel had answered.

"Oh well, you know. I was never very academic." That was a lie, but in the fabricated life of Dariel Hale, this was true. "I couldn't focus at school and never found any joy in anything other than the arts. So, being the stubborn man I am—" (true for all four iterations) "—I only put effort into things that made me happy. And I never stopped." Dariel made a 'hmm' sound, taking another sip of water for something to do. "Now, you must understand, a lot of it was luck. Being at the right place at the right time, but it worked out." *Luck, yeah, sure.*

Godwin looked at him like he'd cured world hunger. "Fascinating, truly *fascinating.* You simply persevered until you made it. Highly admirable, especially in this day and age." He was being genuine as well.

"I suppose, again, I am very stubborn." Dariel tried to dull down the adoration he had received. He wasn't good at taking compliments. "What about you, what do you do for a living? Especially to own a home like this."

"Oh, well. It's a long story, actually." Godwin shifted uncomfortably, his heart rate increasing slightly.

Dariel cocked his head. *Why so secretive?* "What about your staff, you can't be alone in a house this size all the time, surely." He decided to take a different approach, asking the only other burning question he'd had since he arrived. The house really did feel *empty.*

Thankfully, Godwin *did* have a direct answer to this. "Oh, I sent them all home for a few days. They don't work for me all the time, besides, I didn't want to overwhelm my guests!"

Two things stood out as being odd to Dariel. It was an honest enough answer, but it only gave him more questions. Why did he send everyone home all at once? Surely he'd stagger it so he at least had *someone* in the building with him. Not that he wouldn't be capable of managing on his own, Dariel didn't want to insult the man, but he must get exceedingly lonely. In a house this size, Dariel knew even he himself would find it overwhelming. So many things to keep on top of—even just dusting alone, there were *how many rooms?*

The second thing, and perhaps the thing that confused Dariel the most, was this: He was under the impression he was to be the sole guest with Godwin this evening. He'd made no prior reference to anyone else joining them for dinner, so unless he was making a general statement about future visitors, Dariel was not the only person he'd invited this evening. And by the manner in which Godwin had said it, it very much seemed to be the latter.

Dariel frowned. Godwin did come across as a trustworthy man, and Dariel had spent his life being exceptionally good at reading people right from the moment he met them, but he couldn't help but feel as though something was a bit *off*.

He immediately wished he'd brought his case into the room with him, realising no one would have come to move it. His throat closed as he noted Godwin staring at him.

"Are you okay? You're looking a little pale," Godwin observed, but not obtusely.

"Quite well." Dariel took a deep breath, palms sweating.

A bell sound suddenly rang through the house, breaking the tension Dariel believed he was single-handedly managing to create.

The front door.

"Ah!" Godwin was on his feet in an instant. "Two moments, that will be our other guest!"

He'd gone before Dariel had a chance to ask anything else.

<h1 style="text-align:center">Chapter Three</h1>

Dariel often wondered where his trust issues began.

His first life ended as an accident—no one was to directly blame, and yet when he awoke again, he blamed everyone he saw for not saving Annette and *little Sparrow.*

He never learned how he was made; had to figure out how to navigate this new world alone, but he blamed everyone he saw for that too. He was lonely for those first few years, kept himself away from the world, because he thought himself a monster.

He sometimes blamed himself for their deaths, even though he wasn't even there when the flames began.

When he decided to 'die' for the second time, he fled the country. He'd spent over a decade learning to live with his losses, working and learning how to survive again, but once he realised he was never going to age, he wanted to start entirely anew.

He'd heard America was the place to be in the early eighties, so he found himself a small home in New England. By the middle of the decade, he'd moved to New York, decided to flaunt his youthful body, and have some fun.

This was where his trust diminished even more. He got to

learn a lot about people very quickly as they invited him into their beds.

Some were kind, treated him well, while many others had him kicked out onto the streets as oblivious and uninvolved partners would walk in and blame him for spreading all sorts of diseases—some entirely made up.

To men, he was their little secret. To women, he was a porcelain doll.

It was an awful time, really. Dariel watched people he'd begun to consider friends die all around him. He watched as the news painted all sorts of false narratives on big screens, communities falling apart. People being thrown out onto streets and denied health care as though they were sub-human. He watched as those in power allowed the AIDs pandemic to spread and spread for years, always prioritising other things, never their own people.

But he also watched communities come together. Rebuild. *Love*, unconditionally. He joined in with marches, built new friendships, and met so many incredible people as the eighties turned into the nineties.

He always blamed himself for not being able to save anyone, though. For not having the power to cure and make things right. He'd been cursed with this condition, but he couldn't share it. Couldn't burden anyone else with the loss of humanity. He refused to take away that autonomy, just as someone had done to him.

Why was he chosen to live, time after time? Why him?

A handful of years before the new millennium, Dariel learned he possibly wasn't alone.

It happened in a flash, one so quick he would always doubt whether he'd been mistaken, and he hoped he'd find, in time, that he was wrong. It was easier that way. But through all the pulses and sounds of the bustling city, that blond haired stranger did not possess a heart.

He was sure of it.

But they were gone in an instant. Oblivious to Dariel's existence.

He couldn't even trust his own mind. Maybe time would naturally take it from him.

Or, time would gift him.

"There we are, make yourself comfortable! Dariel, this is Athens. Athens, meet Dariel. Dariel is to be my personal designer, and Athens, you are of course going to help me make this house look and feel like a home again. I'm glad you could both make it. I'll let you two get acquainted!"

Godwin was in and out of the room as if his life depended on it. His cheery self left barely a shadow behind him as he closed the door, leaving Dariel alone with the most beautiful man he'd ever seen.

It was a quick and bold realisation—he was aware of that. But his anger at Godwin for neglecting to inform him of this guest was immediately quelled the moment Athens stepped through the door with straight, shiny black hair with red strips flowing past his hips. He had piercing light blue eyes ringed with the blackest eyeshadow known to man, and his full noir ensemble of vinyl, low cut jeans, and a buckled vest top over mesh clung tightly to his slender frame. But the gentle, and equally confused expression painted on his face as he entered eased Dariel a tad.

That, and the fact Athens was dead.

Like him.

Dariel swallowed the lump in his throat, watching the embers light up the side of Athens' body as the other man stood staring at Dariel, reading his face, and forcing Dariel to readjust himself on the chair, worrying he perhaps did not look his best. The tension was again only hand crafted by Dariel, as a moment later, Athens burst out into laughter.

What? Is there something on my face?

Athens threw himself on the chair opposite Dariel in a severely relaxed manner, tightly crossing one long leg over the other and stretching his arms around the back of the sofa, owning the room.

His eyes did not leave Dariel, and a warm pool formed in Dariel's stomach; his lungs forgetting how to function. He took in the other man's body once more, noting a swirling floral pattern under the mesh of his left arm. He wondered if it was part of the material or inked into his pale skin. An abundance of silver jewellery adorned the man's whole body, clinking as he shifted in the chair.

Then Athens spoke. A voice so smooth and calming when he asked, "Do you think he knows?" His eyes shone like turning diamonds, and Dariel noted the gap between his front teeth.

Dariel leaned back as panic and overwhelmed sensations infected every bone in his body. His breath hitched as he opened his mouth. "I've never met anyone like me before." He gulped to ease his throat.

Athens cocked his head, then his face dropped slightly, and he leaned forward, lines of tension in his brow. "What? Really?"

"I...no. Never."

"Who made you?" A question no one had ever asked Dariel Hale, or any of his iterations, yet it flowed out of Athens as if it was the simplest of curiosities.

Dariel's chest constricted once again. "I... I don't know. I never saw... I—" *Flames. Burning. Burning. Burning. Everywhere. Forever.*

Athens' brow loosened in sympathy as he leaned his elbows on both his legs, sincerity radiating from his exquisite form. His chest rising and falling normally.

Relax, John. Just breathe, my beloved.

Dariel shook his head vigorously before the shadows came, then sniffed in, pressing fingertips below his eyes just in case. "Sorry. Yeah. Wow. This wasn't expected. At all. It's been a, well, it's been a very odd evening for me so far."

A ghost of a smile tugged at the corners of Athens' mouth. "I take it he didn't tell you I'd be coming? He didn't tell me you'd be here, either."

Keep the conversation normal, come on.

Dariel sighed out a relieved laugh. "It seems he has kept a lot of things secret."

"Tell me about it. I get an email asking me to come here to help plan out the interior of his home for an exceedingly pretty amount of money, but now looking at the size of it, I feel as though I should have pushed for more." Athens had a sweet laugh.

"I wonder what the urgency is, he came across pretty desperate," Dariel said, trying to sound casual.

"Wild, really. Mid-life crisis, I reckon. I wonder if I'll get one of those soon." Athens picked at his nails, then looked up through his lashes to see if Dariel was looking.

All Dariel could do was gawk as he took in Athens' form for the third time, fully enamoured.

"So do you think he knows, then?" Athens continued to look at his black nails, silver rings adorning each finger. Silver always bothered Dariel, made him turn out in a horrible, burning rash. *Always burning.*

"Huh?" He hadn't processed Athens' words.

The other man looked up, cocking a brow. "About us? Who we are?"

"Surely not."

"A coincidence, then?"

"Definitely." Dariel gulped again, noting the lump in his throat was there to stay.

Athens shrugged then relaxed back into the chair once more. "Stunning building, right? I wonder how he wound up here."

Dariel chewed at the inside of his mouth. "I tried to ask him, but we didn't get much of a chance to talk, I've only just got here myself."

"That was your bag in the lobby? I thought I could sense the blood. Fox, right?"

Dariel nodded.

"Hmm. His staff haven't been doing their jobs then." Athens laughed, and Dariel wanted to join in, but it only made him more unsettled.

"They're not here," he blurted out.

At this, Athens threw him a puzzled look. "What do you mean?"

Dariel straightened his back, choosing to lower his voice for some reason. "The staff. He sent them all home for a few days. We're the only ones in the building."

Athens made the shape of an 'oh' with his mouth, his face tense. "How odd."

As if on cue, footsteps sounded in the hall then Godwin re-emerged, an oven glove on one hand and a metal spoon in the other, twirling it around like a magic wand. "Gents! Forgive me, dinner may be a tad longer than anticipated. It appears I am not the chef I once was. Sorry to keep you waiting."

"That's okay, Mr Peters, we were just getting acquainted." Athens was quick to respond with charm, turning on the chair with his arms crossed over it in the comfort of an unruly child.

Godwin bowed his head, hastily breathing in. "Oh, wonderful." He cleared his throat, his eyes shooting wide open. "Oh, I'm so sorry, I forgot to offer you a drink, Athens! How rude of me. Gosh, you can tell I'm not used to guests. Can I get you anything? Oh, and please, call me Godwin, did I not already say that?"

Athens politely declined, insisting he would wait until dinner, and after a brief glance to Dariel, Godwin nodded his head again, flustered. "Oh, right, okay, well, in that case, you both could erm... it's a big house, please feel free to have a look around. Just, erm... the downstairs. I've not quite organised upstairs yet." He left in a flash, missing how Athens squinted and screwed up his face as he slowly turned to Dariel, who was tensely on the edge of his seat in confusion. Athens laughed once more, breaking all tension. "He's an odd fellow, isn't he?" he said.

"Quite," was all Dariel could add.

'He's quite a handsome gentleman though, don't you agree?'

'What? How are you... you're in my head?'

'You've never experienced this either, have you?'

'I... no. How are you...'

'Have you never controlled anyone? Made a human bend at your will?'

'Yes, of course. It's necessary.'

'So how come this is a shock to you?'

'Please get out of my head, it hurts.'

'I'm not in your head.'

Dariel choked out a breath, eyes bursting wide.

Athens stared at him, waiting for his panting to stop.

"Gosh, you're so tense, you don't need to fight it, you're making it hurt. You just need to relax a little. I'll show you. Come on, let's go and have a wander, I'm intrigued to see what he's got hidden in these walls."

Athens winked and reached out a hand as a thousand butterflies erupted inside Dariel's stomach.

Chapter Four

They retraced their footsteps down the corridor, Dariel taking extra note of the height difference between the two of them, and the confidence in which Athens walked—*strode*. He walked as if he owned the hallways, his head held high with a permanent grin on his face. Dariel was always self-conscious of his height, and this moment was perhaps the worst he'd felt in a while as he struggled to keep up with Athens' pace. He kept looking at the other man in admiration as they passed the oil paintings Dariel could almost envision Athens being a part of.

Dariel had too many questions, his mind ablaze.

They reached the lobby area again, and Athens took charge of their destination, briefly nodding to Dariel's untouched case.

"I say we try this corridor first then work our way back." Athens pointed ahead of them to the west wing of the house.

Dariel nodded, but it wasn't enough for Athens, who rolled his eyes. "Have you forgotten how to speak?"

Dariel startled. "Oh, no. Sorry, I zoned out a bit."

"Do you do that a lot? Zone out."

Why is he asking?

'It's okay, I do too.'

"Please stop that."

Athens sucked in his cheek. "I can't read your mind, you know. We're not that powerful, I only pick up on the stuff you want to hear and make you hear it. You just have to relax and let me in," he said. "It's not quite the same as our ability of mind manipulation, people like us can sense this kind of thing coming. We can welcome it." Athens lowered his gaze. "I can read your body language though. In fact, I'm very good at interpreting someone's thoughts based on how they present themselves. So maybe I *can* read your mind." He winked again and Dariel's breath caught. He'd only done it twice, but each time it made Dariel feel things he'd tried to shut down for a while. He didn't enjoy being distracted and caught off guard, and Athens was already doing a remarkable job at that.

He decided to change the subject, eyes catching the large window in the middle of the main stairs. "Should I maybe move my bag, to keep it out of the way? You know, just in case."

"We're not allowed up there, remember? Top secret mess."

"Yeah, we're both not buying that, are we?"

'We'll find out what's up there in a bit.'

This time, Dariel felt his lips quirk and Athens silently stared at his face with the same expression, eyes twinkling.

Dariel chewed the inside of his mouth. "I'm stressed it's left out in the open."

"You have a lock on it, right?"

"Yeah, but..."

"Then there is no problem. He can't go snooping. But if it will put you more at ease, you could move it to the side of the staircase so it's more hidden." Athens reached down to take the case, and it was only then Dariel realised he'd already gripped the handle himself. Their arms brushed, and Dariel caught the scent of mint as Athens came up close, silky black hair sliding over his shoulders as he bent forward.

Dariel dropped the handle and watched Athens lift the case,

resting it against the staircase wall beside a giant, mahogany-rimmed globe. A black rucksack was already lying there, which Dariel deduced belonged to the man at his side.

"Better?" Athens raised a brow, though not unkindly.

"Yeah," Dariel breathed out.

"Great, let's explore." With that, Athens reached out an arm to gently squeeze Dariel's shoulder, sending electric sparks through every inch of his body.

Oh, dear. Dariel thought, turning his head so Athens couldn't see the way heat rose to his cheeks. *It's been a while since I felt that.*

The pair of them headed down the hallway and entered through the first open door to the front of the house, flicking on the light. The living room, it seemed. Or at least one of them.

Like the hallway, the room looked untouched. Preserved in time, waiting for visitors to peer at it from behind velvet ropes. *Don't touch, no flash photography, keep the line moving.*

The room was a mixture of baby blues and greens. A grand fireplace graced the far corner with a large mirror above it, spanning the entire chimney breast wall. Three floor to ceiling windows stood adorned with navy, crushed velvet curtains, trimmed in gold, letting in the blackness beyond. An exquisite, gold chandelier hung in the centre of the ceiling, making rainbows from the light.

After a low 'wow', Athens snorted. "I wonder when the last time he sat in here was."

"Probably the last time he had guests," Dariel joked.

At that, Athens turned and looked down to him, sucking in his bottom lip, eyes merry. "You're probably right."

They quickly moved on to the room opposite, which was behind a closed door this time, but as Dariel opened it and Athens switched on the dim and buzzing light, they understood why. It was merely a storage room; a single wooden table stood in the centre with two large, chipped-paint wardrobes on either side, one door slightly ajar. Boxes upon boxes of varying sizes, all nondescript, were piled on the floor and table, some open, most sealed. There was a damp smell emanating from them. Dariel grimaced.

"How long has he lived here?" Athens asked sincerely from the doorway.

Dariel stepped forward out of curiosity and peered into one of the open boxes on the table. "He never said, but I figured a while," he answered as his eyes met with a dozen dead flies and he pulled his head up fast, turning to face the door. "Odd bloke," he muttered. *Were his cleaners never allowed in here?*

Athens shrugged his shoulders and headed back into the corridor.

Dariel followed and caught Athens inspecting the trim along the wall for dust with his finger, his eyes wandering up to the wallpaper.

"Have you ever lived in wealth this grand?" Athens asked without taking his eyes from the wall, deep in thought.

"Of a sort," Dariel said.

Athens flicked his attention back to Dariel, face unreadable in the dim light. "You're a fashion designer, right?"

Dariel gulped, he didn't really know why. It was as if the question held a different meaning, but he quickly deduced it was probably because talking to Athens was something he'd never experienced before. Talking to someone like him rewired his brain a little, he'd forgotten how to act normally.

"Yeah," Dariel sighed. "For now."

Athens scowled. "Meaning?"

Dariel straightened up, then the honesty poured out of him. "I'm coming to the end of this little life. Time to move on soon."

Athens pouted in concentration. "Huh," was all he said.

"What?"

"How old are you?" Athens stepped towards Dariel.

"Twenty-four," Dariel blurted out upon instinct. Then inwardly frowned at the blatant lie, adding, "forever."

Athens walked even closer now, shoulders relaxed. "You look younger, honestly."

What was that meant to mean?

"That's a compliment, by the way," Athens flicked his head. "I died at thirty, so I just about saved myself from an eternity of wrinkles."

Nothing wrong with age lines. I find them quite attractive, actually.

"I'm joking, of course. Godwin suits them. I'm too punk for mortality."

Dariel raised a brow, multiple questions firing through his head at once.

Athens flopped his arms down, tilting his whole body to the side as he laughed. "Another joke, gosh you really need to chill out."

That offended Dariel, but he realised the other man had a point. They were both just as much in the dark as each other, and they were both *the same*. He was probably the safest he'd ever be in Athens' company—despite still not truly knowing him at all.

"Sorry, you're right." Dariel relaxed his shoulders.

'No need to apologise to me.' Athens stepped over to squeeze Dariel's shoulder again, his thumb lingering a tad longer this time, stroking the crook of Dariel's exposed collarbone, lighting up his body once more. Then a burning sensation appeared as the tiny slip of silver from Athens' thumb ring finally reacted with Dariel's skin, immediately fading as the connection broke. He almost flinched, but instead he just nodded, itching away the feeling the same moment Athens turned back around and headed further down the hall.

"We can maybe get to know each other properly now, yeah?" Athens asked as he walked further and further away, Dariel's feet refusing to carry him anywhere.

Athens reached the door at the very end and turned the handle; a warm, amber glow illuminating his face as the room greeted him in. "Nice," he said before disappearing into the mouth of light.

Dariel hurried to join him, turning into the room, and grinning with pleasant surprise. It was a small study space with a large sofa along the closest wall, and a desk with papers scattered all over. The carpet was worn and the chair cushions were flattened with age. It felt *lived in.*

Athens was already crouching over the desk, rummaging through the pages and drawers.

A floorboard creaked as Dariel joined his side. "Woah, should we be doing..."

Athens stopped him with a stern look. "He let us roam, it's his own fault for leaving this room open. Plus, I want to know more about him, don't you?" He looked up through his lashes in a way that cut off any words Dariel had ready to say. Another well-made point.

"What about the other room, though? He might have stuff in boxes that could..."

"This room smells nice. It wants to be used."

Dariel huffed at the absurdity, reluctantly joining in.

They didn't find anything interesting, unfortunately. Just dull government documents and bills with a few architectural plans buried amongst them. A handful of documents they found thankfully proved Godwin did in fact have a gardener, a cook, and at least three cleaners, which was comforting knowledge, but also begged more questions over how secretive Godwin must have been with certain things in the house. With three practically full-time cleaners, he must have deliberately told them not to go into certain rooms. Which means he either really was hiding something, from more than the two of them, or he was just a really private man.

"I was kind of hoping to find some really incriminating documents, but I suppose he wouldn't be stupid enough to leave that stuff out." Athens tucked his hair over his ear as he leaned over the table, the red streaked length of his mane tracing over the wood. Dariel smelled mint again, noting once more how close the pair of them were.

Athens didn't seem to mind, though, so Dariel didn't move.

"He might actually just be a shy man who wants to jazz up his boring life," Athens surmised, the vinyl of his trousers sticking slightly as he switched his weight to his right leg. Dariel, for the umpteenth time, found himself glancing over Athens' full body. The deep arch of his back, and the smooth, delicate bobbing of his neck as he swallowed. Athens turned to face him suddenly and Dariel took a step back.

"You find anything?" he asked, but Dariel knew Athens was aware of what he'd been doing.

"No, not really." Dariel spoke too hastily for his own liking, dropping himself into Awkward Land.

'Like what you see?'

Athens straightened up before he gave Dariel a chance to respond, eyes scanning Dariel's face, really not helping at all. His eyelids drooped. "I'm only messing with you. Here, let's take a seat. Talk a bit. I want to get to know the famous Dariel Hale."

Athens ushered them both to the long Chesterfield against the wall, sitting himself on the far corner and giving Dariel plenty of space to choose from.

"You know my full name?" Dariel questioned, sitting down with enough space between them to make it less uncomfortable for *him.*

Athens held up his hands. "Guilty," he said before relaxing back down into the arm of the chair. "I'm actually quite a fan of your work. Still got one of your jackets from the late nineties. I was trying to make conversation."

He knows me?

'Long-time fan, my friend.'

Oh.

"So what made you decide to start designing?" Athens inquired as a genuine fan would.

Dariel leaned forward, comfort loosening his muscles. "Oh, well, I've always been into wanting to wear things that stand out, not in an egotistical way, more a freedom way. Going against the norm." For the first time, that question hadn't annoyed him.

"I get that. I mean, look at me." Athens gestured to his own attire. "I was hardly my grandmother's favourite child."

Dariel chuckled at that. "Are you... like, into the *goth scene* or something?" *Asked the sixty-four-year-old grandfather. Nice one, Dariel. Really showing your age there.*

"For now." Athens shrugged, a smirk forming as he watched Dariel's eyes intently.

"How old are you, really?" Dariel's confidence was in full swing now. He was pleased it was back, he'd missed it.

"Ha. I see you calculating. I'm forty, as of a few weeks ago. A baby, really. This is the only life I've lived, technically. Which is... not the same for you, I'm guessing?"

"I'm sixty-four."

Athens' eyes widened. "Wow. So you're actually older than Mr Mystery," he gestured down the hall with his thumb.

"I presumed I was."

Athens was fully intrigued now, leaning on both his knees. "Can I ask how many lives you have lived then?"

Dariel sunk in on himself, but brushed it off. "I was meant to start life number five a week ago, but this email threw my plan off track."

Athens didn't speak for a moment, then he brought a leg over his knee. "You were going to disappear? Begin again?"

"Dariel has done his time."

Athens' brow furrowed. "So you...what, move away and start fresh?"

"It's got to be done."

"But your image, you're well known. You're in magazines, you've appeared in fashion shows!"

"It won't be as easy as it has been in the past."

"How were you going to do it?"

"Death, naturally."

"Makes sense. Something theatrical, I assume?"

"Dariel enjoys a drink. It was only a matter of time before it caught up with him."

"Fitting. Who will you become?"

Dariel blinked hard. "I hadn't really thought about it, I was just going to see what happened. I quite fancy France this time."

Athens nodded. "Interesting. And you've really never met anyone like us?"

Dariel shook his head. "Never. I woke up this way forty years ago and yeah... I've been alone." *Change the subject.* "What about you? I'm sorry I was never well versed in the interior design world, are you well known?"

Athens' eyes widened and he clutched his hand to his chest with a feigned shock. "Nice insult," he gasped.

"Oh, no, sorry. I didn't mean it that way, I'm sure you've been doing amazing, I only meant like..."

"Not many people know my face, no." Athens dropped his head with a grin.

After a brief pause, Dariel adjusted his trousers, angling himself more towards his new friend. *New friend. Could he be one?* "How long are you going to stay in this profession, do you think?"

"You mean, when will Athens Daněk perish in a god-awful accident and find himself in a vineyard in Italy?"

Dariel smiled.

"Funny you brought up your own story, because it was the email that stopped me from becoming a column in the local newspaper too."

"The industry is so draining. You come in and out of relevance at the click of a finger." Dariel let his thoughts flow.

"Tell me about it!" Athens agreed enthusiastically. "God, it's a nightmare. I'm lucky I can leave it whenever, and I kept telling myself I could go when I wanted to. My dad's no longer around, I have very few memories of my mum, and I've not spoken to my sister since I... well, she won't miss me, let's just say."

"I'm sorry," Dariel found himself saying.

Athens batted a hand at him, pursing his lips. "Don't be, I'm a lot happier now. What about you? No one to miss in this life?"

"I learned a long time ago to never bother getting too close to anyone. It makes it easier to let go."

Athens nodded in slow understanding. "Fair enough."

"Plus, up until today, I thought I was the only one with this condition. I could never tell anyone what I was, so I might as well have lived in blissful solitude."

"You're not alone now, though." Athens' voice was solemn, but laced with comfort.

Dariel looked up at the other man. "No. I'm not." He swallowed hard.

"We're in a cool mansion with a very excited rich man who is going to pay us nearly a quarter of a million pounds. Could be worse." Athens lightened the mood.

"And he's invited two immortals into his home." It was Dariel's turn to wink now, causing Athens to react smugly.

"That he did, that he did." Athens pushed his body up and flicked his head back in the direction of the door. "I wonder what he's cooking up."

"Hopefully something I can stomach. I've never been good with real food."

Athens scrunched his nose, sliding back into the chair. "Me neither, not as fun if you can't chase it."

Dariel gawked and Athens once again burst into a fit of laughter. "A jest, all a jest, darling. I'm actually extremely lazy. I think I've rid the entire forest behind my house of grey squirrels." Athens crossed his legs again, the vinyl sticking. "Which, I've heard, might actually help red squirrels return. So, in a way, I'm helping out the animal kingdom."

"Have you ever fed from a human?" Dariel startled himself with his abruptness, but he didn't regret the question. He wanted to know more about Athens, quite desperately.

Athens took in a breath. "A handful of times. Only because I was new to it all, and I'd seen one too many horror movies. I never killed a human though. Just... you know... quenched my thirst."

"I killed someone. Once. Accidentally." *Wow, I'm getting too comfortable now.*

Instead of asking for more details, or looking even remotely shocked, Athens stretched his hands out and said, "great, at least I know who can take matters into their own hands if this job turns sour."

'*What an odd thing to joke about.*' Dariel attempted to force the thought into Athens' head, causing his own to hurt.

'***Dariel, darling, you've never killed anyone who didn't deserve it.***'

'*What? What makes you...*'

'***I just know it. I told you I'm good at reading people.***'

Dariel took in a deep breath, surveying his surroundings before turning back to face Athens, and let a cold nothingness wash over him as he opened mind again, trying to relax as much as he could.

'*He deserved it.*'

'***Thought so.***'

Despite being stunned, Dariel also realised this meant he was one step closer to opening up fully, laying all his cards on the table. Letting someone else in. Maybe it was because of their circumstances. They'd both lived a kind of life very few others will ever experience. Casually admitting murder was, in every other circumstance, wrong. Not this time. Not with Athens. A man he'd only just met, but someone he needed. This was comfort in relatability, and it was nice. Really nice, actually. Relieving, even.

It was also not lost on him that this was the second time

Athens had casually called Dariel 'darling' which... did something to him. Something he thought he maybe quite liked. He wanted to hear Athens say it out loud again. Hear the word roll off his tongue as he looked into Dariel's eyes and leaned closer so the scent of fresh mint would encircle them both and...

"What's with the shadows, then? I've never met someone like us who has such an overwhelming energy around them."

Dariel's lungs closed up as he blinked deeply, brutally shaking himself from the thoughts he was working his way to, instinctively turning his face away before clearing his throat and staring at the floor. *Of course Athens noticed them.* "Oh, they're erm..."

Athens shifted on the sofa, his voice growing slightly lower. "Oh. I'm sorry, I got too comfortable. Forgive me, you don't have to answer..."

"Just memories." Dariel shot back up, a tear threatening to drip from his left eye. He wiped it away quickly. "Memories." He smiled away the flames. *No one has ever seen them.*

"It's good to hold onto memories. We're going to make a lot of them." Athens reached out his hand to almost touch Dariel's thigh on the sofa. An offering of support.

"Yeah. You're right." Dariel nodded, trying to rebirth his confidence.

"Just... well. Don't let them consume you."

You don't know me, you... Dariel felt a defensive streak of anger deep inside. Athens read it immediately, leaning back.

"Sorry, that wasn't my place. We barely know each other, after all."

"It's okay. I'm just... I don't want to talk about certain things." *Calm, Athens meant no harm.*

"That's okay. I get that. I'm quite a private person too, believe it or not."

Dariel didn't know how to respond, he just looked at Athens' pretty face and let his lungs expand a few times.

"It's nice to finally meet you, Dariel Hale." Athens stood up and thrust out a hand. Dariel was about to take it, but noted the rings and hoped his eyes would explain for him. Athens immediately understood, pulling all five rings off and shoving them into his pocket. Dariel took his now bare hand, the other man's skin warm and soft.

"It's nice to meet you too, Athens..."

"Daněk." Athens reminded him politely. "It's Czech, though I unfortunately speak very little. We moved here when I was young and my dad insisted we... It's actually my mum's family name but, well... never mind, we don't need to discuss that right now." He sighed, not dropping their hands.

Dariel tried not to look too solemn. "Nice to meet you Athens Daněk. I should look into your work, I might take some inspiration."

"It would be an honour, I'd be happy to show you any time." He still did not let go of Dariel's hand, even as they lowered them; the connection warm and protective.

"If we make it out of here alive." Dariel huffed out a laugh.

"If indeed. Now..." Athens dropped his hand finally, the connection gone in an instant. "What do you say we have a look upstairs?"

"We're not meant to..."

"Precisely, darling."

<h1 style="text-align:center">Chapter Five</h1>

Dariel was never really one to break rules, believe it or not. If it could be helped, he'd rather not make a scene. But he decided to make no objections as Athens led him up the grand staircase, once again passing old portraits and random ornaments from eras clearly predating the house itself. The thick, red carpet was well looked after, Dariel noted as he looked down to watch his step, preparing for the inevitable floorboard creak to expose them. None came however—they successfully snuck up with a great silence.

The landing didn't look messy, in fact, it was quite the opposite. It was *too* clean. As in, it *smelled* like someone had freshly painted the skirting boards, and dusted and vacuumed very recently. Each branch of corridor led to multiple closed doors, and a vase was placed in front of the sash windows on either side. Perfectly positioned with precise symmetry.

Dariel sensed Athens coming to the same conclusions as their eyes wandered over the pristine, Victorian, paisley wallpaper lining the walls. The pair of them stood side by side in equal confusion.

"Yep, the guy is definitely hiding something."

His wife in the attic. No wait, which book is it where...

'Jane Eyre. We're his replacements.' "Come on." Athens

wasted no time, charging head on towards one of the doors, tapping Dariel on his lower back as he did so.

Dariel shook his head to stop his few seconds of delay before he walked over to the door Athens was already struggling to open.

Athens pulled back and sighed, flicking his hair back and placing his hands on his slim waist, agitated. "Bloody locked!"

"Definitely a body in one of these rooms." Dariel tried to make light of the situation to appease his growing fear that maybe—just maybe—they weren't safe here. Sweat pooled on his palms as he made small fists down by his side.

"Why would you lock your own doors unless you had something to hide?" Athens added after trying the door again, huffing with frustration as he failed.

Dariel decided to try the other corridor himself, twisting the nearest doorknob. After a brief moment of annoyance, he realised it was just stuck. A little shoulder strength forced the door wide open.

Athens was hot on his trail, coming right up behind him immediately. The room before them was exactly what Dariel expected—a nondescript bedroom, untouched and infused with the scent of a stately home.

"His bedroom?" Athens questioned, his breath tickling Dariel's shoulder and sending a pleasant tingle down his back.

He needs to stop being so...

Dariel cleared his throat. "Not his bedroom. This room hasn't been touched in a while," he observed.

"Hmm," Athens muttered, pushing himself into the room to examine further. He immediately threw himself onto the four-poster bed in the centre, and bounced back as if checking into a hotel.

"Hey! We probably shouldn't start disturbing things too much," Dariel heard himself saying before he truly had time to consider what he actually cared about.

"We've already disregarded the one rule he gave us, as long as we don't break anything, we'll be fine," Athens stated from the bed.

Dariel edged slightly further into the room, hands still clammy, but he convinced himself Athens had a point, and he was quite enjoying the snooping. The theorising. The company.

"Definitely not his room, you're right," Athens noted before sneezing three times.

Dariel could help but chuckle. "You okay, there?"

Athens sat up, eyes blinking wide. "The mystery cleaners missed a bit," he joked.

"Maybe this was one of their rooms?" Dariel surmised, stepping over to one of the windows and looking out onto the grounds below.

"That would make a bit more sense, but it also looks too 'someone died here and we're keeping it as a shrine', don't you think?" Athens' nose twisted.

Dariel turned to face the other man still sitting on the bed, letting his fingers brush through the velvet curtain, mind deep in thought. "Or maybe he doesn't actually live here at all."

Athens raised a thick brow and Dariel noted the way the man was positioned on the bed: Long legs widely parted and feet firmly planted on the floor. Slender arms rooted at either side of his beautiful body.

Beautiful. What the hell am I...

"What?" Athens tipped his head to the side, and Dariel immediately realised how awkward he'd made things. His arousal filled the room like smoke.

Athens played into it, parting his legs ever so slightly wider and leaning back. Their eyes met and neither of them looked away.

"I erm..."

"You think he's pretending this is his home?" Athens asked the question very calmly, as though the past minute had not happened, but his posture did not change, and his eyes were still glued to Dariel. He wobbled his knee a little. *A tease.*

Dariel snapped his gaze back to the window, his face was definitely a shade he really didn't want anyone to see, and his trousers grew tighter around his crotch.

Jesus Christ, Dariel. Stop this. You know how desperate you look right now? Pull yourself together, lad.

"Oh, this is his home, definitely." Athens had somehow managed to glide silently over to Dariel's side and planted an elbow on his shoulder, Dariel being perfect height for an arm rest. His body seized up as the pair of them looked straight outside.

"I don't think we're here for the reason he gave though."

How is he staying calm? He knows exactly what he's just done, how can he be so casual and move on like...

"And I think we might find out soon."

Then Athens' presence vanished, and Dariel watched the reflection of the other man leave the room. A choking weight leaving Dariel's shoulders.

"Hey, hey, wait, what do you mean by that?" Dariel finally broke out of the *moment* as Athens' statements lingered in his brain, and he darted out of the room after him. He was aware of his raised voice as he found himself back on the landing, slamming his hand over his mouth abruptly, as if it would have made a difference.

Athens was back at the other door, resting on one knee as he stuck a hair pin through the keyhole, and rattled the handle again. Dariel came up to his side, the *moment* gone.

Athens didn't look up from his focus as he spoke. "I just meant he's being too 'nicey nicey', and he hasn't really given us a lot of information to make us trust him. I mean, look..." Athens tutted, not giving up with the clearly locked door. Dariel wasn't quite sure what he was hoping to achieve.

"The email he sent us. It was out of the blue, and too good to be true. We both think that. Yet we both needed the money, so we said yes, without *really* thinking about it. He told neither of us we'd both be here at the same time, he sent all of his staff away for the week—that's if they even work for him anymore—and then he lets us have a look around his home but *not* the upstairs, which he wants to hide from us for some reason. We're all strangers here, but he's brought us together on purpose." A sigh. "All I meant was, we need to pay close attention at dinner, and ask him as many questions as we can. If it turns out he's secretly a homophobic serial killer who wants to rid the world of attractive queers, then we kill him first, and go to the papers with our story."

Dariel just blinked. Athens noted his silence and flicked his head up to him, a smirk forming on his pretty face.

He is pretty. Oh, John. You are allowed to think that.

"What? Sorry, did I assume wrong? Or was it the murder part you didn't like, cos we can try ulterior methods if push comes to shove..."

"You think I'm attractive?"

Athens stood to full height, inches away from Dariel, heat radiating from his skin. Dariel drank him in, his black trousers shaping his slim legs, the smooth skin stretched over his visible collar bones poking up from the buckles, and belts, and...

"Of course I do, darling. I'm a long-time admirer, as you already know." Then Athens' face dropped as Dariel stayed frozen in place, his mind a million miles away from focusing on what his face might be showing.

"Have I made things weird?" Athens asked, stepping back slightly. "I do have a tendency to be a bit full on."

"I just..."

'Oh, the shadows. I'm sorry. I'm sorry, Dariel. I didn't mean to make things weird. I should have known not to...' Athens stepped back quite far, almost as if he was suddenly *scared.*

Dariel couldn't *feel* the shadows this time. Maybe they weren't even there... *Maybe he's read between the lines I didn't even know I'd given him.*

"I'm gonna look down the hall to see if..." Athens' throat

bobbed, eyes filled with shame. Dariel cut him off by reaching out and grabbing his wrist, holding him in place.

"No," he said, confidently. "You don't have to stop."

Athens' brows knit together, tension lifting a notch. "What?"

"I find you attractive too."

Dariel actually *felt* Athens' whole body relax this time. The other man stopped pulling away and moved back towards Dariel, looking down in sorrow.

"You're charming, and cool, and maybe it's because you're the first person I've met who is like me so I could just be intrigued by you, or maybe it's the adrenaline or fear and confusion of our predicament, but in the very short space of time I've known you, I know I want to get to know you more, and whatever happens tonight, I'm kind of looking forward to spending more time with you." Dariel let out a deep breath, then allowed himself to look up at Athens, pleading. "If you'd want that?" *A friend? Or something more?*

Athens stayed silent for a beat.

Dariel continued. "And I don't mind the way you're acting around me, I'm just..."

"You don't have to explain. I shouldn't have been so forward."

"It's just been a really long time." Dariel finished off his confession with a laugh of relief, hoping it would ease Athens.

It did the trick.

"Okay, okay. I get that." Athens bit his lip. Dariel resisted the urge to slap his arm playfully, maintaining a grin instead.

"I need to see what's in this room." Athens professionally changed the subject and went back to the sealed door before them, this time peering through the keyhole. Dariel came up to join him, bending down to his side and immediately scenting the mint again, this time mixed with... *eucalyptus*?

"I can't quite make it out, but there's something fancy in there. Gold perhaps," Athens said, almost muttering it to himself as though he was trying to calculate something. "I've never had the best eyesight, can you..." He shuffled back, hinting for Dariel to take his place, and he did, filling the space and peering into the hole. He was very aware of the position they were now both in, Athens hovering a gentle hand to Dariel's side as he whispered close. "Anything?"

Dariel surveyed what he could. It appeared to be another bedroom, but a heavily ornate one in comparison to the one down the hall. All blues and golds, an indistinguishable but grand mural of birds and flowers on the far wall where the extremely large bed stood. And the room was lit, with a sense of atmosphere, perhaps by lamps and candles, as opposed to a large overhead light. It seemed very much lived in.

'What do you see?'

'He definitely does live here.'

'His room?'

"Gentlemen!"

'Shit.'

The pair of them shot up, startled by the bellowing voice from below.

'It's okay, he can't really do anything. We'll play it off.'
Dariel nodded.

Godwin shouted again, this time from slightly closer as it was clear he'd begun to climb the stairs.

The pair began to descend, meeting their host in the middle. He didn't look angry, but Dariel read something behind his eyes that indicated frustration.

"Did I not ask you to stay downstairs?" Godwin questioned them both, though more in the manner of self-doubt. They could convince him he forgot, Dariel thought. Athens was perhaps already on it.

Godwin began to smile, his whole manner shifting. "No matter, gents. Dinner is ready, come join me in the dining room!"

And that was it. Godwin gestured towards the direction of the room. Both Athens and Dariel kept their spirits high as they headed down, Athens in front.

'*Close.*'

Dariel imagined him winking and kept his head down.

Chapter Six

For about six years, Dariel did have a friend. A companion. Someone to turn to. Shirley, her name was. The pair of them shared a terraced house flat with two other occupants in mid-seventies York. She was the only person Dariel—who went by Kit at the time—would let get close, because he believed them to be similar, immortality aside. She worked as a nurse in the city centre, and would often come in from night shifts in the early hours of the morning, precisely when Dariel would prefer to go hunting for food. It was a frequent occurrence that he was up in the shared kitchen when she'd get in. At first, he'd thought it was going to be too much of a problem, that she would begin to grow suspicious of him, but she would always smile at him and never questioned why he was up—to the point where he began to learn her schedules, and would have a cup of tea ready for her when she got in.

The pair would chat a bit, she had an infectious personality, and before long, their conversations started turning more and more personal. He learned about her difficult family life, and why she moved away from the south as soon as she could. In turn, he shared about his wife and *Sparrow*. She was the only person on planet earth who knew his story. Even though he changed the dates to avoid suspicion, it was the most he'd trusted anyone with.

"You carry them with you, don't you?" she said once, pulling her steaming mug to her lips, maintaining eye contact.

"I suppose I'll never let them go. They're part of me."

Shirley smiled at him sympathetically.

A few years went by, then Shirley began bringing her boyfriend to the house, and would occasionally leave him to roam when she went to work. Dariel found it uncomfortable when he'd bump into the man and often kept his head down—but Shirley had shared enough about Dariel to him that it didn't take long for him to start calling for Dariel when he was around.

Dariel was always a slight man—struggled to build a lot of muscle, and only being five foot six on a good day meant Shirley's boyfriend, who was easily a good few inches over six foot, would tower over Dariel's space in quite an unsettling way.

"Hey, mate, I wanna talk to you." It took three attempts to ignore him before one day Dariel decided he would have to get their interaction over and done with, for Shirley's sake.

On the day Dariel obliged, the pair took a seat in the kitchen. It was about an hour after Shirley had left for work and time for Dariel's evening meal, but he figured he would get the conversation out of the way.

It started off as a normal 'getting to know my girlfriend's close friend' conversation, but slowly his voice grew firmer, and at some point he started leaning over the table slightly—asserting his dominance. Dariel had expected it. You know, a pretty young woman's best friend is a single young man who lives in the same flat as her. It didn't matter how uninterested Dariel tried to present himself around Boyfriend, it was clear he wasn't buying it.

The conversation ended with something along the lines of 'stay away from my bird'. Dariel had almost opened his mouth to inform Boyfriend that women are in fact not animals, but he found he quite enjoyed having naturally straight teeth, so upped and left in silence.

Dariel was quite content with leaving Boyfriend to bathe in his own fragile masculinity for as long as Shirley wanted him around, and he had even considered moving out, just to make things easier for all of them, but then came the shouting. It was a Victorian building, with thin 60s divider walls, and Shirley's bedroom was right beside Dariel's. Sometimes he'd hear raised voices and would listen in. It was normal for couples to argue, but in that manner? He thought of Annette, and how neither of them had so much as glared at each other in their six years together. Maybe he was just lucky. People fight. They argue. This wasn't any of his business.

Until it was.

Dariel made it his business.

One day, he waited up in the kitchen for Shirley, knowing she'd be alone, but she never returned home. She hadn't said she'd be staying with Boyfriend, which would have been fine, simply a miscommunication. When she did turn up, three hours later, she'd hurried up the stairs, ignoring Dariel's call. He went up after her, banging on her door. He could hear her moving about frantically on the other side.

"Shirley?" he called, trying not to sound too aggressive.

There was no reply. He tried calling again, then finally, after his third attempt, Shirley flung open the door and stood there in nothing but her tights and a vest top; mascara staining her cheeks and rimming her bloodshot eyes.

Dariel took in the bruises, working his eyes across her body. Her *whole* body. Her arms were battered in shades of green and brown, marks in various stages of healing, and though he couldn't see them, his eyes homed in to the various bruised pulses across her abdomen and thighs, even the back of her head, covered by her tattered, mousy brown waves.

"Shirley..." he breathed out.

"What do you want?" she snapped, the remnants of tears in her throat.

"How long has this been going on?" Dariel's gaze darkened.

"He doesn't... it's not as bad as it looks."

"How long, Shirley?"

She clamped her mouth shut and gulped. "He gets frustrated sometimes, he doesn't mean to. He's had a hard few months. He..."

"How long has he been throwing you around like a worthless rag doll? Using you as a punching bag? Raising a fist to you in... has he—"

"Never. Kit, I promise. He's never done that to me... it's just..."

"Just what? A one-sided boxing match?" He practically shouted this, and immediately regretted his tone, watching the fear swim in Shirley's eyes.

"Enough! Please, Kit. Please. I..." then she burst out crying and when Dariel lifted his open arms to hold her, she flopped her head onto his chest and relaxed into his embrace. She felt tiny in his arms. He didn't want to tighten his grip too much, but he wanted to support her, to let her drop her full weight into him if she wanted to.

How dare he. Dariel thought as her sobs soaked into his shirt, his gaze fixed out of the window in the flat where the sun was beginning to peak through. *How fucking dare he.*

Then there was only rage. Something Dariel hadn't experienced since he woke up to ashes.

Boyfriend's body was found in the woods a few days later, time of death recorded as being specifically when Shirley was miles away at work. As it turned out, she wasn't his first victim. At least she would be the last.

Dariel was already in America by the time the news started reporting it though. The shadows followed him as always.

He deserved it.

"Please, take your pick where you'd prefer to sit!" Godwin beamed as he opened the dining room door; the medieval style table extravagantly set before them with a velvet runner, candelabras, and an abundance of exotic fruit and vibrant, multi-coloured flowers. To the right were leaded floor to ceiling windows that could open out onto the front patio, and to the left, a deep oak wall with various different pieces of historical artwork. A large, low hanging, diamond chandelier lit up the centre of the room, beaming down onto the table below. For a table that size, Dariel thought it odd there were only four seats; two at each end, facing each other meters apart, then two in the centre. All places laid out with three sets of cutlery and cloth napkins, all rolled and held in place with large silver rings.

"I'm impressed," Athens said, striding into the room with his hands clasped behind his back. "I fear I am a little underdressed, however." He made his way to the seat in the far corner.

"Nonsense, young man. You look delightful." Godwin chuckled to himself as he indicated for Dariel to pick his own seat.

He went for the seat closest, making Athens at least two meters away from him. Godwin hovered over the heavy chair between them before turning and walking over to his illuminated alcohol cabinet in the corner of the room.

"Red or white, gents?"

Dariel glanced at Athens from over the table and Athens shrugged.

'You pick.'

'Red?'

'A classic.'

"Erm, red please, Godwin."

"Excellent! An excuse to pull out my finest Merlot." He began to mutter to himself as he opened the bottom of the cabinet. "I've had this bottle for years, it's too fancy to have all to myself."

'Years. He's been alone for years.'

'Maybe he just means dinner guests.'

Athens threw a sidewards glance to their host then sat back as Godwin appeared at his side and began to pour into his wine glass. Athens nodded graciously.

Godwin then waltzed up to Dariel and did the same. Dariel noted a pleasant scent radiating from the other man as he came close—something he couldn't remember smelling before. A fresh, almost lavender scent? His host smiled at him gently, and Dariel was almost taken aback with his own reaction. *He is not bad to look at, at all.*

'Some might say a silver fox.'

'Stop!' Dariel glared at Athens who only smirked and sucked in his lower lip, having already taken a sip of his wine.

'Again, I'm only reading your body language.'

'Well, please stop it. It's distracting.'

'What's distracting, me or him?' Another wink, Godwin none the wiser.

Their host cleared his throat, which thankfully saved Dariel from having to mentally answer Athens' teasing comment.

"Right, onto the starter it is! I do hope neither of you are allergic to anything," his open face dropped, "I probably should have asked beforehand."

"I'm fine," Athens confirmed, looking to Dariel for his own response.

"Same for me, nothing." Dariel smiled.

"Excellent. Three prawn cocktails coming up!" He bounced off to the kitchen and Dariel resisted the urge to continue grinning as Godwin passed. He was such a charming fellow. *He seems so normal. What could he possibly be hiding?*

"Remember what we agreed on," Athens said into the silence, taking another large sip of his wine. "Ask him *everything*. We'll know when he's lying."

"Will we?"

"Just ask. We'll be fine."

We'll be fine. We.

Godwin returned and served out the delightfully displayed starters, finally seating himself and pulling out a napkin to push into his collar, shuffling on his chair in an excited manner. Dariel waited for both Godwin and Athens to take a mouthful before attempting his own, then waited for the conversation to naturally commence, hoping his companions would start.

"So, Godwin. How did you find yourself living in a place like this?" Athens asked after a mouthful. He'd tied his hair back to keep it out of his face. Even from the distance he was sitting, Dariel noticed how fine Athens' bone structure was. Sharp cheekbones but a soft brow and jaw, *the best of both* he found himself thinking.

Godwin straightened his back and his lips disappeared behind his moustache. A brief glimmer of melancholy passed over his face before he turned to Athens with a smile. "I'm afraid to admit the answer is rather dull. It's in the family, this was passed to me many years ago."

"Impressive, so you've always lived in wealth then?" Athens continued casually.

Godwin cleared his throat again. "That's all I've known. Though..." he paused, perhaps considering the wording of his answer, "I wouldn't say wealth equates to happiness, I hope you understand."

Not the reply Dariel was expecting, but it was the most they'd gotten out of the man thus far.

"What do you mean by that? If you don't mind me asking?"

Athens was not letting down. It was rather like an interrogation now, Dariel observed.

Godwin's brow furrowed a little and he dropped his miniature fork to the table. "Well, you know. Money doesn't buy happiness, it's a common phrase, I'm sure you've heard…" Godwin trailed off, adjusting his chair.

"I understand what you mean, Godwin," Dariel said, garnering the attention of both men as he spoke. "I came into quite a bit of money about ten years ago with my work, and you think at a time when you don't have it, it will sort everything out in your life. It is the cure to everything that could possibly ail you, both mentally and physically. But you find out rather fast that actually, it changes nothing."

Athens kept looking at Dariel, gaze softening.

"Yes. Yes, that's exactly it." Godwin relaxed again and picked his fork back up, pointing it towards Dariel as a prop of expression. "It is quite sad, really."

"A fact of life," Athens bluntly stated, leaning back into his chair, and knitting his fingers together over his stomach. He'd finished already.

"I actually began to give most of it away to charities. It was only right, since I hadn't really earned a penny myself," Godwin continued.

That pleasantly surprised Dariel, but Athens cut in with his next question before Dariel could dwell. "What sort of charities do you support?" he said. *'Here we go.'*

"Well, quite a few." Godwin dabbed his mouth with his napkin. "Mainly ones for, erm. LBGT… erm… sorry." Godwin's eyes rolled up as he mouthed his mind calculations. "L.G.B.T sorry. I'm terrible with acronyms, forgive me."

Dariel watched Athens' eyes widen as his own did the same.

'Never mind. Let the man speak… that was entirely unexpected.'

The three of them sat in silence for a moment, Dariel clanging his fork to his plate before the air choked him.

"You're..." Athens started. It was clear he really had been thrown off guard.

Godwin nodded to himself, sitting back. "I've been donating for years. I, well, it means a lot to me."

Dariel sat still, his mind whirring with memories and all the struggles he watched people go through. All the hate and lies thrown at him and everyone else over the decades. *Dirty queers. It's unnatural. You're going to hell.*

"If you'll excuse me," Godwin suddenly stood, scraping his chair back over the polished floor and lifting his plate. "Are we erm, are you both finished?"

Dariel wasn't quite done, though he could never force himself to eat too much solid food, especially when he was nervous, so he politely accepted as Godwin reached for his and Athens' plates then hastily disappeared out of the room.

Athens shot up the moment the door swung closed and strode straight up to Dariel, placing his right hand on Dariel's shoulder; eyes wandering around the room as he spoke. "Okay, we've definitely misjudged him, big time. I'm..."

"Lost for words?" Dariel looked up to the other man, whose bare, elegant fingers were still pressing into his shoulder. The fluttering in his stomach returned.

Athens finally planted his eyes on Dariel, but his gaze was still distant, his mind too active. "Yeah, I'm..." he bent down and lowered his voice. "Do you think he's like us?"

"Queer or dead?" Dariel tried to joke, it was the best he could do.

Athens' shoulders loosened again, and he dropped his hand, face wandering back to the door behind Dariel's chair. "We made him uncomfortable. Well, *I* did. I really am a little full on sometimes."

"It's okay." Dariel remained as calm as he could in his chair.

"We'll change the subject, quiz him about the invitations, and work out if he really does still have staff." He shut his mouth. *'Keep the conversation light and humorous and he's bound to let it slip without us having to do a great deal.'*

'I could convince him to tell us everything.' Athens' tone came across slightly skittish still.

"No. We don't need to... it's not right. He doesn't deserve that." Dariel made sure his voice sounded confident and assertive as he spoke aloud once more. *It wouldn't be fair.*

Athens didn't speak for a moment, away with his thoughts, then he patted Dariel twice on the shoulder and turned back to his seat. "You're right."

They did not talk again until Godwin re-entered the room, serving Dariel first with a steaming plate of pie. Despite the strong, hot food smell, the lavender was even stronger. More overpowering than before, as Godwin brushed his side.

He's trying too hard.

Once everyone was served and re-seated, Dariel could finally note the subtle change in Godwin's demeanour. He had this new air of confidence about him, as though the jolly but shy man from before had disappeared behind a mask. Or was this now with the mask removed?

Godwin prepared his cutlery, tucking the napkin back into his shirt. "Shepard's pie. Exactly how my mother used to make it. It's my favourite, I couldn't resist." Those were still his words, but the life-filled energy he spoke with earlier was missing. He now spoke more matter-of-factly. An off-putting tone of sudden professionalism.

"It's been a long time since I've enjoyed a Shepard's pie, thank you," Athens returned the formal tone.

"Yes, thank you, Godwin," Dariel added before pretending to tuck in. He was beginning to feel rather sick at the thought of eating.

"So, gentlemen, we should probably discuss the business at

hand!" Godwin spoke after an eternity of silence between the three of them. Athens didn't even look as though he wished to speak, he just tucked into his meal like a child starved. *He's a much better actor than me.*

"Design, fashion, galore!" Godwin sounded more like a merry businessman now, having downed his second glass, and opening the fresh bottle of red he'd brought over before beginning his meal. Rioja this time.

Athens finally looked up. Straight at Dariel.

'Here we go. Now comes our chance.'

'You want me to start?' Dariel gulped at the realisation, then leaned forward, thrusting all remaining confidence he had into his words. The headache grew less and less the more he let Athens in. He'd been resisting too much before. Their mental communication was growing more natural now.

"Yes, well actually, we, well, *I* was wanting to ask you a few questions before we start." His hands were shaking. *Why? You're in control of this entire situation. You're the oldest, most experienced, you need to start thinking higher of yourself.*

"Ask away." Godwin smiled, dabbing gravy from his mouth.

"Well... for starters... I..." *Just speak.* "I was wondering why you didn't mention Athens in the email? I thought we were to be alone?"

Dariel caught Athens' brow rising from the corner of his eye, but he kept his own eyes on their host.

Godwin looked mildly puzzled, not quite understanding the statement. "Would you have preferred us to be alone?"

Hands in your hair.

Strong fingers pressing into the flesh of your thighs.

Dariel blinked hard, startling himself back to the present. *It's been so long.*

He refused to look at Athens.

"No, sorry, I didn't mean it in that way, I was just surprised to learn you hadn't only invited me."

"Oh." The mask slipped. Godwin's face dropped to the table then he coughed, his voice quieter and gentler: "Well, I must apologise on that front. I had neglected to include clarity over how this evening would play out."

"It's not a problem, Godwin. Dariel and I have found great company in one another." Athens finally decided to join the conversation, though Dariel couldn't quite make eye contact with him still.

Godwin paused before he smiled, his aura dimming.

'The best company.'

'Took your time.'

'You don't do this a lot, do you?'

'What? Accept invitations to secluded manors from strangers?'

'Talk to people.'

'Well... I. Hey!'

Athens winked at him, and Dariel really did almost stop breathing.

How does he do it? Get through to me like that? And so easily...

Godwin coughed once more, which finally clicked in Dariel's mind that it wasn't a cough of illness, no, this was an awkward habit. He was nervous. Had been from the moment he opened the door. *But why? He invited us.*

"You must understand, gentlemen," Godwin started, "I wasn't quite sure either of you would respond. I've been in need of your assistance for a while, but had to take my time making sure you both were specifically who I needed, and I truly was ready to contact you. It is a big ask from both of you, and I expected to be ignored, so I didn't want to come across too desperate in the email, choosing to keep it simple. And also..." Godwin dropped his gaze again, one of his hands having moved to his lap. Another sign of his genuine shyness. "I thought perhaps you both already knew each other."

Dariel tilted his head subconsciously, trying to understand. It was a plausible excuse, though it had thrown him how he'd presumed Dariel and Athens were already acquainted. It didn't seem that way when he'd introduced them earlier on.

Athens put his knife and fork down, swallowing his last mouthful. "I've been a long-time fan of Mr Hale's work, but it has always been admiration from afar. We don't even live in the same city," Athens confirmed.

How does he know where I live?

'I'm pretty sure the whole fashion industry knows you live in London, darling. Don't worry.'

Dariel straightened himself out, pulling a lump of mascara from his lashes.

"My mistake then, you do appear to have gotten on well already. Perhaps you both just have good taste," Godwin said, sounding almost pleased with himself. "How is the food?" He asked at exactly the same time Athens blurted out with: "How many staff do you normally have?"

Dariel responded with gratitude to Godwin's question, though his host had immediately turned towards Athens' bluntness.

"I'm sorry?"

Athens did not stutter: "Your staff, how many do you normally have working on the house? The gardener, chef, cleaners?"

"Oh," Godwin said again, sinking inward. "I suppose I was a little vague about that earlier, and I owe you the truth."

Finally, we're getting somewhere. Dariel sighed.

Athens stared at their host intently, awaiting the response.

Godwin blinked seven times to the ground and folded both hands together.

He's terrified...

"I erm... I let them all go."

Dariel scowled at the same time Athens' eyes widened.

"You fired them?" Dariel awaited clarification.

Godwin turned his attention to Dariel with solemn eyes, his

kind face stoic but soft. His heart had begun to speed up at some point in the last few minutes and Dariel homed in to it. Homed in to every aspect of the man. The nervous twitch to his shoulders, the neatly trimmed beard woven with moonlight, his shining emerald eyes behind the bold framed glasses. Godwin had been nothing but a saint to them since they arrived. Dariel was looking at an ordinary man, but one holding onto many secrets. A man afraid.

"Fired sounds a tad harsh. They did nothing wrong," Godwin said softly. "I decided I no longer needed them, so I found them jobs elsewhere. This was only a few weeks ago." His eyes did not leave Dariel.

"So you've been entirely alone since then?" Dariel felt a sadness sweep over him.

Godwin almost laughed, disguising it as a smile. "I'm more than used to being alone, Dariel. I have been most of my life."

Dariel let himself fully focus into the conversation with Godwin alone in that moment. He tried so hard to read the man, his chest constricting as he did so. "You chose this?" *Why can't I figure him out?*

Godwin subtly nodded. "I don't think anyone *wishes* to be alone in this way, but sometimes that is how life must be. It was for the best. They were good friends to me, but they deserved to be out of this prison. It's too secluded, it wasn't fair on them. I manage quite well on my own..."

"You see this place as a prison?"

Godwin did laugh this time, properly. He set his hands upon the table. "It is a prison of my own making, nothing more."

"What are you punishing yourself for? You could leave at any time, you could move anywhere you liked. Go out into the village, meet people. Meet a partner, perhaps?"

The brightness faded from Godwin's face. "I have no need for a romantic partner. That is the way I am, the way I have always been."

Dariel's brow furrowed. "You don't have to be alone because you don't want romance. There are infinite kinds of connections you could have! You could experience so much, live life to the fullest. Do whatever your heart desires!"

"I do leave the house, you know. When I need to."

"I don't think you leave enough!"

"Dariel." Athens' firm voice broke the shield around him, crashing him back into the dining room, where he had always been. He took in his surroundings once again and breathed in and out deeply. He'd gotten carried away.

'The shadows. I can see them.'

'Oh. I...'

'Don't apologise, just breathe. We barely know this man. You barely even know me.'

'I think I'm beginning to.'

Athens sighed. *'I know. As I am learning you. Perhaps we are all not too dissimilar.'*

"My apologies, Godwin. It appears I'm a lot more exhausted from my journey than I thought. Forgive my abrasiveness."

Godwin nodded, seemingly unfazed. "It is quite alright, Dariel. You are not the first person who has said such to me, and I do hear you. I appreciate your concern." He took another mouthful of his mashed potato.

Without thinking, Dariel reached for his napkin and pulled the ring from it—sharply dropping it as a sting sung through his body and he let out a yelp. It was pure silver, and he had already noted that, so why had he been foolish enough to forget already? *You're not thinking straight.*

At the clatter, both his companions darted their heads towards him. Athens understood immediately, Godwin's face unreadable.

Dariel laughed it off. "Sorry, I accidentally poked myself. Sharp knives, I mustn't be trusted with them." He attempted a joke, but he sensed Athens' smirk and deduced he'd taken it too far, making a meal out of it.

'You're such an idiot, you know.'
'I'm well aware, thank you.'
'It's cute.'
'Oh, stop.'
'Endearing.'
'Please.'
'Hot.'

At that, Dariel did blush. A warmth pooled in his belly, and he instinctively turned to the windows to his right.

"Are you okay, Dariel?" Godwin asked, his genuine concern apparent.

Dariel flashed him a smile. "Splendid."
'Smooth.'

Chapter Seven

The three of them continued to eat their meals, Dariel trying to be discreet about everything he did after his little outburst. He wanted to put himself into silent mode—to stop being perceived. But all the while he ate, head kept facing the table, he thought of Godwin living alone in this house, no one to talk to, nothing to do, and doing it willingly. When he tried to focus on something else, his mind immediately wandered to Athens, and the image of how he sat in the bedroom pinned itself to the front of his mind.

Athens' warm breath on your neck, what those long fingers would feel like on both your shoulders. Bare shoulders.

Athens pressing you into the wall. Skin to skin. Hands running down your bare torso to the button of your trousers.

Then Godwin appeared at the door in his mind, and the image faded a bit until his gaze focused in on Godwin's form, then it was *his* firm hands on Dariel's shoulders and he felt a tug behind him as Athens brushed back his hair and planted a delicate kiss on his neck and—

"So, Godwin, what drew you to our work?" Athens asked.

He didn't sense my mind wandering. Good. Dariel flushed,

keeping his head down. He wasn't ready to unpack those thoughts, his body had other ideas though.

"You both have a rather unique flair, and I was wanting quite a drastic change to my entire image. Call it a mid-life crisis." Godwin spoke with a calm manner once more, his nerves almost entirely settling.

"Were you wanting a full house redesign? I couldn't help but notice you keep a lot of your doors shut," Athens persisted.

Godwin scrunched his lips as if considering his answer. "Hmm, perhaps. Though some of those rooms are closed for a reason," he finished firmly.

And the reason? Dariel looked up from his food, eyes shifting between the two men.

"You let me know what things you had in mind, I will need to take some measurements first, of course. Get the floor plans to make some sketches." Athens didn't push the topic for once, though it seemed to Dariel that was intentional.

Godwin nodded and ate a forkful of peas, then turned to Dariel, his eyes sunny. "And you, Mr Hale, have the task of making me look... *cool*." There was a smidge of humour in his tone.

Dariel awkwardly mopped his mouth. "I will try my best."

"Then you can start frequenting town as the most fashionable man in Oxford," Athens added.

Oh, that was clever.

Godwin winced. "Perhaps I will have to."

"You don't want poor Dariel here to design you an entire new wardrobe, only for the only people to see it being the Victorian ghosts in the halls now, do you?"

Godwin looked like he'd been shot in the back. "You've seen ghosts?" he asked, severely panicked.

Athens looked equally shocked for a moment, then sank back, entertained. "Oh, no, that was meant to be a joke." He mellowed. "Is this place *supposed* to be haunted?"

Godwin shook his head, taking another sip of wine. "No. I do not believe so. You may hire a team of investigators who will claim the place is riddled, but I've never experienced anything that could not be explained. Thankfully," he added as his eyes blanked.

"I'm terrified of the concept of ghosts." Dariel thought it helpful to inject into the moment.

"That makes two of us," Godwin said. "The last thing I want in my home is unwanted guests."

Overthinking was Dariel's speciality. *Does he mean he is sick of us?*

"What do you enjoy doing then, in your spare time? A house this size should surely have some entertainment gems." Athens was swift to keep the topic from wandering.

"I do read a great deal. I'm sure you already guessed that from the library room I invited you both to earlier. That's my favourite room to frequent. It brings me peace." Godwin closed his eyes briefly, reminiscing. His mask was well and truly falling now, and the bubbly man who opened the front door hours ago had returned.

"I used to read a lot of fantasy when I was younger, a bit of horror too, which probably comes as no surprise." Athens gestured to his own attire. "Once a goth, always a goth."

"I loved the goth scene when I was younger, I should let you take a look through my record collection, they're all stacked up in one of the rooms upstairs. My record player broke a good few years back and I never had it replaced—you might find some stuff you like, and you can take whatever you want."

Athens' eyes widened like a child's on Christmas morning. "Oh, are you sure? I wouldn't want to take anything valuable. I have a friend who is good with fixing up old stereos and vintage electronics. I could get him to take a look at your player if you want, and you can relive your youth!"

Godwin swatted a hand. "Oh, there's not much point, it was far beyond repair even in its final days. Besides, I'm too old for that stuff now."

"You're not too old at all. There's no such thing as being too old to enjoy things, anyway." Athens almost looked offended. "I'll get you back into enjoying these things, just you wait." Athens winked at Godwin, and for a millisecond, a wave of jealousy slapped Dariel in the face. *Stop this, you hardly know either of these men. It's only a month-long job, you may never see them again afterwards. Athens is free to flirt with whoever he wants.*

"Oh, Mr Daněk. You flatter me, but truly, I was never made for standing out."

Athens' voice dropped. "I can help with that too," he promised, sheepishly.

Godwin chuckled, his shoulders bouncing up and down. "I didn't have the confidence then, I sure as hell do not have the confidence now. Please, take what you like, I insist."

Athens looked defeated, slumping back into his chair.

"And you, Mr Hale, you have free rein of my clothing collection. I have no use for the majority of it anymore, you may find some antiques." Godwin spoke as if they'd suddenly known each other for years. Like old friends catching up. It was comforting and helped to dissolve a lot of Dariel's initial doubts and questions, but he could not fully let his guard down yet. The life of Godwin Peters was still a great mystery.

"I must say," Athens finished his drink, wiping his mouth, "you are quite a gracious host. You've gone above and beyond this evening."

Godwin blushed, his full cheeks beaming. "Oh, well. It is all or nothing with me when it comes to dinner, I'm afraid. I couldn't expect you both to travel this far for mere mediocrity." He set his knife and fork on either side of his plate. "Besides, you both turned out to be exactly who I hoped, and it has relieved me massively, I will admit. I can often be very reserved. More wine, Dariel?"

Dariel was stunned out of comfort, hiccupping. "Oh, sorry. Yes, please." It was his turn to clear his throat now. As Godwin stepped towards him, heat returned to his belly, and the scent overwhelmed him. Godwin looked into his eyes and Dariel refused to look away, fixing his gaze upwards towards his host as he poured.

"You're a bonny fellow, aren't you," Godwin said as he stepped away and wandered back to his seat, causing Dariel to take a sharp breath. He felt Athens' gaze burn him from across the room, the attention of both men wholly on him.

"Oh, thank you." He never got used to compliments, since they were often laced with judgement, no matter how kind they seemed.

"Easy to spot in a crowd," Athens added.

Godwin must have seen the mild discomfort wash over Dariel's face. His eyes drooped slightly. "I meant nothing but the utmost respect there, Mr Hale. I was drawn to your uniqueness. In fact, I quite envy you." Their host reassured him. "There are many things I wish I'd been brave enough to do in my youth. I often wonder if I have perhaps wasted my life, looking back now."

Dariel scrunched his nose. "What do you mean?"

Godwin sat back, shuffling on his seat like he'd already said too much. "Oh, well... You know. I'm not exactly, erm..."

His shyness was endearing to Dariel. He was a man of many secrets, but now, Dariel believed he'd be learning many of them very soon, one way or another.

'I am growing to enjoy his company, aren't you?' Dariel tried his hand at being the confident one this time. He watched Athens reach up to rub his top lip.

'Not usually my type but he is growing on me. What about you?'

Dariel thought back to his past partners—both sexual and platonic. No one ever lasted that long. He spent most of his time on his own after all, but the time he spent in the beds of others were mostly happy memories. His escape from reality. When he could be himself. No strings attached.

He took a deep breath. *'He's very much my type.'* He was being honest.

'Hmm. Interesting...' Athens didn't look up.

Godwin could have changed the subject entirely if he'd wanted. The ball was in his court, but instead, in those few short minutes, he'd thrown away his mask and became his true self. "Gentlemen, I... may I ask something from you both?" He had finished his meal, napkin removed, and he tousled his grey-brown hair back. "It's not quite what I ever thought I would ask—not how I pictured the evening going—but now that I've spent an hour or so with the pair of you, you've given me the confidence to open up a little. That's if you don't mind. I understand this was meant to be professional business and this will turn rather personal but I..."

"Go ahead," Athens said with his hands under his chin.

"Yes... I don't mind..." Dariel added much quieter.

Godwin breathed in deep through his nose and puffed out his chest. "Oh, grand. Okay. Well. Here goes. Now, stop me if this is too much but... How did you both, how would I put it, learn to love yourselves? Your life. Who you are?"

A dribble of wax spilled out from one of the candles onto the centre of the table.

Athens spoke first. "As in, our careers or..."

Godwin bit his lip before throwing both his hands over his mouth. "Oh, God. No. Never mind. Forget I said anything. More wine? How was the food? We can discuss business in my office if you'd prefer..."

"I had a wife once." Dariel blurted out, eyes glued to the candle wax. No one spoke, but he knew they were both listening.

"Annette. We married young and bought a small cottage with money we'd both saved up, with some help from her parents. She was everything to me, and I mean *everything*."

'Oh, Dariel, you don't have to...'

Dariel filled his lungs, gaze still distant. "I loved her with every fibre of my being. With Annette, I was invincible. She never talked me down, never judged me, never forced me to do anything I didn't want to, and I did the same for her. We went everywhere together—had our whole life planned out."

'The darkness, Dariel. I can see shadows.'

Dariel closed his eyes, forcing bravado into his voice and shoving all the whirring thoughts down as deep as he could. *Don't stop. You can't stop now.*

"When she died, I thought I'd never speak to another human again. I thought I would be going behind her back, keeping secrets from her. Anything I did without her felt like I was lying to her. I suffered with my own mind for years. In a way, these thoughts may never leave... but after a while, I thought about what she would think if she saw me being the way I was. Unhappy. Miserable. Forcibly alone." Dariel finally looked up, locking eyes with Athens, whose own eyes were glistening.

"I started to experiment with fashion. Started raiding charity shops and putting together outfits I felt good in. I had this confidence rise in me for the first time in years. I mean, at first I was too embarrassed to leave the house in them, afraid of what people might think, and it took me a while to get out of that mindset, but over time I told myself there was no more use in hiding. I will admit, being in the public eye has given me a lot more protection than many other people like me, so I will not say it's easy, but it's not us who must change, it's other people."

Athens slowly nodded; Godwin didn't move.

"I have been with both men and women in my lifetime. I heard the whispers, I endured the pain, but they never stopped me from being who I was. How could they? There is nothing wrong with me."

'There is nothing wrong with you at all, Dariel Hale. You are a marvel.'

"My family disowned me after I came out," Athens started. "They thought I carried the devil in me, and the only way to rid their household of evil was to banish their own flesh and blood onto the streets. My own little sister began making up disgusting rumours about me and essentially cast me out of the entire village. Love thy neighbour and all, what a load of bollocks."

'*I'm so sorry, Athens.*'

'**Don't be. It was their loss.**'

"I moved away and stayed in and out of my friend's flat for over a decade. I got jobs here and there, did what I could, and found my own apartment, but then I had a bunch of medical expenses. I kind of needed someone with me through the various processes, so she insisted I stayed with her until I could live alone again. She encouraged me to start my own business, the dream she knew I'd had all my life. So I did. I worked and worked, and eventually I started my own company. Everything fell into place. Everything happens for a reason, right? Well my life couldn't have gone any better. I didn't have to do any of the hard work of leaving, my family did that for me. You could say I found it quite easy to be myself, but others might not see it the same way."

Dariel accidentally placed his wine glass atop a spoon and made a clattering sound.

"Was that what you meant, Godwin?" Athens asked softly, undistracted.

They both watched Godwin's throat bob, his eyes darting between the pair of them.

"Oh dear. I..." He fidgeted with his hands on the table, uneasy.

"I suppose that might have been a bit much," Dariel said.

Godwin shook his head. "Oh no. I am grateful you shared your stories. I can only apologise for encouraging you to share if you were perhaps not expecting to." He kept looking at them both as if observing a tennis match.

"Are you..." Dariel started, but Godwin broke him off.

"I am a gay man. Yes. I'm... Wow. I..."

"It's okay, whatever you wish to say will stay in this room, right Dariel?" Athens said.

Dariel nodded. "Of course. We wouldn't have shared such

personal stories with a stranger if we did not feel comfortable in your presence."

More than comfortable. How did this happen so fast?

"I have not forgiven myself for what I did. I never will. I..."

"Again, we cannot really judge, after all, we all only met for the first time this evening. If you wish to get something off your chest, you have the best company to do so with. You're sitting in a room with two people like yourself."

Godwin nodded his head towards Athens.

'He's crying.'

'What? Really?'

'Almost.'

Dariel scratched his head.

'Quite an evening this is turning out to be, hey?'

"I was born into wealth. It is all I've ever known. Summers in one home, winters in another. My only obligation in life was to carry on the family name and make my parents proud." Godwin straightened his back. "I have both brothers and sisters, older and younger, so I never believed the expectations put upon me would ever be truly enacted. I knew from my teens I did not like women, not in the way my brothers did. I thought perhaps it was just a temporary issue with my brain, a delayed response, but as I grew older, I found the feeling was not going away. I wanted to sleep with men, I wanted them in my bed, but I never wished to marry or to become romantically involved with anyone... it made no sense to me. I thought perhaps I was wired wrong."

It had begun to rain outside again, and the wind battered at the large panes to the right of the room, branches scraping and tapping. They let him continue, no interruption necessary.

"In my twenties, I met a man. It was the early seventies, what we both wanted wasn't just frowned upon, it had not long even been made legal. I'd grown up knowing our very existence was a criminal offence. But we both wanted the same things. Sex, and friendship. Nothing more, nothing less. We managed to keep our engagements secret for years. We made it work, understood it could end at any point, but we were happy. We satisfied each other's needs perfectly. We didn't require anything else from each other. I thought I was the luckiest man on earth—to have not only found a truly incredible partner, but also a friend who understood I could not and did not experience any sort of romantic attraction. He didn't expect anything from me." Godwin's gaze grew distant with the memories. "Then my brother caught us. I never did get on with my eldest brother, but I will never forgive him for what he did. Even though what was to come was entirely my fault."

Still, neither Dariel nor Athens spoke. Phantom hands tightened their grip on Dariel's lungs.

"He told my whole family, even exaggerated and twisted what he'd witnessed to make me out as a true monster. I was immediately given a choice: leave him and repent—to force him away and never see him again, or be cut from the family entirely. My money and name would be stripped from me. As you can see," he gestured around to the room, "Godwin Peters chose greed."

Godwin closed his eyes and sighed. "So here I am. I chose this, this was the life God planned for me, and here I sit confessing to two strangers after eating my favourite meal as if it is not something that kept me up at night for decades. As if I am still loved by everyone related to me. I know now I am perhaps not broken, and you gents have helped solidify that to me, but it is too late for me to do anything about it."

"It's not your fault," Dariel asserted.

"Oh, but it is, my dear. I chose this house and my own family name over the life I truly wanted for myself. I chose the worst option, and my family still won't even talk to me, and thus, this is my penance."

"A life of solitude? A life of staying away from everyone as *punishment*? You could have gone back to him! What was his name? I'm sure I could find him, I..." Athens' sudden burst of seriousness shook the room. He'd stood up, hands firmly on the table.

Godwin cut him off with a raised hand, eyes glistening in pain. "I believe he found himself a partner not long after I left him. We were never romantic, but I believe he found his romance and is in fact very happy now."

"Yet you are not," Athens stated, firmness still present, though he did not sound like he was shouting *at* Godwin that time, more shouting *for* him. He sat back down.

Godwin didn't respond.

'He's more than not happy. His whole life has been modelled around one mistake.'

'I'm not quite sure I know what to do.'

'I think we need to help him.'

And I think he asked us here for that exact reason. Dariel couldn't shake the feeling. He chose to trust his gut.

"Godwin. Why did you invite us here?" he asked, stoically.

"Well I..." Godwin swallowed, adjusting his glasses. "I told you, for designing my..."

"Why are we really here, Godwin?" Dariel tried again.

Godwin abruptly stood and clattered back over to his alcohol cabinet.

Athens scowled in confusion then turned to face their host, Dariel doing the same.

Godwin rummaged for a while, bending down on his knees that subsequently cracked as he did so. He reached to what appeared to be another door inside the cabinet, hinges squeaking, and a small light beaming. A mini fridge perhaps? They watched him sigh and drop his head into his hands, muttering to himself.

'What is he doing?'

'I'm concerned.'

Dariel raised to stand. "Everything okay, Godwin? Mr Peters?"

The human did not respond.

"Honestly, I'm a bit full of wine, we don't have to..." Athens started, standing up and beginning to wander over to Godwin.

Then the older man raised slowly, holding up a dark bottle.

The sinking sensation began then, though it took Dariel a further few seconds before his brain caught up.

Godwin's eyes were red as he stepped back towards the table, the unlabelled bottle grasped firmly in his hands. He took in a deep breath, and neither Dariel nor Athens moved; Dariel noting Athens' tense body.

Godwin nodded to himself before he spoke, twisting the bottle cap.

"Time to crack out the good stuff!" It almost didn't sound like the man at all. Godwin's heart racing too fast for a healthy pace. He was trembling. Eyes forced wide.

'Dariel.'

'I know. I don't…'

"Dariel, your glass?" Godwin turned to him, and if he were not already dead, Dariel would have collapsed with fear.

He stayed silent, eyes fixed to the bottle.

'It's human.'

'I know. I…'

It was a bottle of human blood.

'He knows.'

Chapter Eight

When Dariel celebrated what would have been his body's fiftieth birthday, he got drunk alone. He went out onto the midnight streets of London and ended up in a bar where he quickly realised, with the last remaining sobriety he had, he was very much not welcome there. He was used to people staring at him, and would often use his ability of manipulation to soften the blow of the stares—making people turn away. On this particular occasion, however, he was too drunk to remember he could even do that. So instead, he stared back. The next thing he remembered, he was in a gutter with a broken nose, an aching jaw, and a bloodied shirt.

Human blood.

That was the last time he let himself out in public *that* drunk. It was too much of a risk. Especially since not long after this event, he signed with his first agent. He was always extremely careful, always cleaned up after himself, both physically and mentally. How could he have been so careless?

Dariel could only think the worst—he'd revealed himself to this person and scared them off, meaning somewhere out there, there was a man who would have woken up and believed he'd seen a monster. Dariel could only pray his assailant was also too drunk to believe his eyes. And pray he did.

***

Godwin's face dropped, though he was still shaking and gripping on tight to the open bottle.

Dariel clenched his fists and his gums ached, teeth threatening to lengthen; hyperaware Athens was in the same boat.

'We should make him forget.'

'I want to hear him out.'

'This is dangerous. Vampires don't get caught.'

'Is that what we are?'

'You don't think so?'

'I've never said it out loud.'

'Well, we're vampires, and he's not, and he's trying to feed us human blood.'

'It's two against one.'

'We can't be known.'

'We already are.'

Godwin looked mortified, as though he had been able to hear what the pair were saying to each other, despite not a single word being muttered. "Oh, gents. I'm sorry. Did I pick the wrong blood type?" He sounded genuinely sincere.

'I don't think he's going to harm us. We should see what he has to say.'

'Famous last words.'

Neither of them moved as Godwin dropped his shoulders and stepped over to place the bottle on the candle-lit table. He closed his eyes and sighed. "I apologise. I didn't know how best to go about this."

'I think we need to talk to him.'

Athens paced towards Godwin, arms reaching out. "Godwin, dear, perhaps we should all sit back down now."

Their host lowered his head to his chest then reached forward to support himself on the table, stretching out his back. "I don't know what to do," he muttered, almost silently.

The two vampires looked at each other, lost for words. Dariel watched Athens' eyes glisten in the ambient light.

'He's terrified.'

'He invited us!'

'I think he's...'

Godwin shot up. "I can't do this," he announced, tears choking his throat as he made a b-line for the door.

'Stop him.'

Dariel darted over to catch Godwin before he made it to the door, grabbing the larger man by the biceps and pushing him back so he couldn't get any further forward. Godwin did not protest, heart racing as he panted out the adrenaline in front of Dariel. Dariel caught their host's eyes and searched for something, anything, to try and read him. All he found was sorrow.

"Godwin," he said softly as his host's arms weakened and he relaxed, dropping most of his weight into the push.

"I thought I'd be strong enough," Godwin whispered as a tear dropped to his moustache, and Athens quietly appeared behind him, reaching out to place a hand on Godwin's shoulder.

Dariel's dead heart ached as Godwin finally pulled back and his breathing returned to normal.

"We're not going to hurt you, but we can't let you leave this house," Athens stated calmly.

Godwin nodded slowly. "I understand."

"Shall we sit down, yeah?" Athens gestured back over to the table, trying to calm the situation.

"I..." Godwin wheezed a cough. "I'd prefer to sit in the library, actually. If that's okay." He looked up through his thick brows at the pair.

Dariel took a deep breath. "Okay."

"We'll have to escort you. We cannot let you leave," Athens asserted again.

Godwin sucked in his lower lip. "Lead the way then, gents."

Athens shut the door tight as Dariel and Godwin made themselves comfortable on the sofas opposite each other, the fire still breathing; giving the room a deeper, redder hue than before.

Dariel sat with his back to the door this time, eyes fixed on Godwin as Athens came up beside him and sat down. Close. Their thighs almost touched, sending a buzz of electricity to Dariel's groin. He attempted to ignore it. *Not now.*

"So," Athens began. "I want you to tell us everything, from the beginning. You think you know what we are, I want to know how, then you need to explain in great detail why you invited the two of us here tonight."

Godwin opened his mouth, but Athens raised a finger. "Ah ah, there is no use in lying, so don't." It was the harshest Dariel had heard Athens be, but it was necessary. He'd already planned his move if Godwin attempted to run.

Godwin pressed his hands between his thighs, rubbing them together with nerves. He looked younger in that moment, Dariel thought. The way the fire embers cast shadows onto every carved detail of his face graced him with innocence.

"We're not going to hurt you," Dariel added as an important reminder.

"I believe that," Godwin began, tone serious, but face remaining that of a mourning angel atop a gravestone. He did not meet their eyes.

"We're all ears then." Athens stretched an arm back along the head of the Chesterfield so his fingertips brushed the shirt on Dariel's left arm. *Not now, please.* Dariel adjusted himself, placing both hands casually in his lap.

"I went about this all wrong, please forgive me. I should have been up front and honest from the start. But then you would not have come, would you? Or you would have perhaps had to kill me for good measure? A swift extraction. I am not daft, I understand I've put myself in danger regardless." Godwin's voice both deepened and wobbled slightly. He looked up at last. "Now I know you both, or at least have begun to scratch the surface of your lives, I do not feel fear. At least not from yourselves."

"Continue," Athens remained blunt, but his arm behind Dariel only gave off comfort. Protection. Athens' fingers wandered up and over his left shoulder.

"I was only ever ninety percent sure. I've had a lot of free time, you're aware of that, and I spent a large proportion of that researching. Random things at first, but for whatever reason, I grew attached to the concept of 'The Vampire'. I did enjoy horror as a youth," he looked up to Athens and grinned, no longer affected by his tone, "and I always believed out of all the fantastical supernatural creatures that keep us up at night, the concept of a vampire existing in the real world made the most sense to me. So I searched to find answers."

Dariel sat motionless, trying to collect his thoughts as the other man spoke. Athens only seemed to be getting closer and closer, despite having not moved another inch.

"It took me years. For years this idea occupied my mind as I read through account after account and stories and documentaries, and I made a list of every trait that could scientifically be explained. Drinking blood was a must, and sunlight made sense, but only to an extent. You cannot simply flake into a million ashes at the slightest touch of sun, so I had to have my wits about me as I searched. Taking all these accounts with a pinch of salt. Most other things I couldn't quite explain—manipulation? Mind control? Possibly, it made sense to cover your tracks, but I couldn't back it up by science. Reaction to silver? Again, it could work, but why? What made you resistant? Then there are matters of the heart. You are undead, are you not? What keeps you breathing? I was truly fascinated by these baffling concepts, and they plagued my mind. I was adamant by this point I would have to prove to myself that vampires existed one way or another, so I never stopped theorising and scouring the internet for every little drop and sprinkle of an answer and I—"

"Okay, you've clearly done your research. I'm impressed with the dedication," Athens cut him off, "but how did you find *us*? What made you conclude Dariel and I were who you were looking for? How did you manage to narrow your search?"

Godwin raised his hands and laughed once. "Well, actually, it was you, Mr Hale." He narrowed his eyes towards Dariel, who thrust himself back into the chair in shock, hand pressed to his chest.

"What did I do?" Dariel asked with a panic. Athens' arm tensed behind him.

Godwin stood and walked over to the fire, prodding it with a poker and laying another log on before he spoke again. Dariel let his eyes wander over the other man's body as the tendons in his forearms flexed, his sleeves having been freshly rolled to the elbows. He didn't have to turn to know Athens was staring too.

"Did you know there is a story out there claiming you're undead?" Godwin said into the flames.

Oh, shit.

How had he gone this long without hearing about this? It was inevitable his slip up would have come back to bite him, this just wasn't quite what Dariel had predicted.

"Go on..." Dariel said, closing his eyes.

"Well, the undead implications came later. Though the initial article itself, or should I say *forum* post, was more indicating your immortality. It appears quite some years after you became relatively well known in the public eye, a woman came forward with an article titled 'It's HALEing Vampires'. A nice play on words, claiming you'd not aged a day since she met you in the early nineties. Harmless really, I'm sure it happens to many celebrities with good skin care routines and surgeons, but the comments underneath were most enlightening."

Oh, here we go. Dariel leaned his left arm up onto the edge of the sofa and caught his chin and mouth in his fingers, feeling Athens shift.

"It is apparently common knowledge your birth year has been tracked to 1971, making you thirty-one at the time of the article, and hitting thirty-six currently. Again, not too much of an issue, as I said, many celebrities continue to bask in their youth well into their forties and fifties. But someone grew quite adamant that was not the case."

"The bar," Dariel said, sighing.

Godwin turned to fully look at him, the embers continuing to cast a pretty glow over his form. "You know?" His brow raised.

"Unfortunately, I believed I'd gotten away with it."

Athens pulled at his shoulder. "You got caught?" He looked at Dariel with a firm scowl.

Dariel ground his teeth in guilt, holding his hands up in surrender. "Possibly."

"How did you manage that?"

"Well I told you Dariel was quite a fan of a single malt, did I not?" Dariel tried to play it off in jest, squinting his eyes and flinching away as Athens playfully swatted him on the back.

"You absolute idiot." Athens shook his head in disappointment.

"It was a long time ago! I presumed he would have forgotten!"

"Are you aware of what this man claimed, Dariel?" Godwin's tone remained quite serious. He stayed standing with the poker in hand.

"I can guess," Dariel said slowly, clenching his teeth again.

"He claims you accosted him in a bar in 1992, then dragged him out into the alleyway and bit him, drawing blood from his neck."

A snort sounded behind—Athens. "Boy are you lucky he said that last part. Otherwise your career would have gone down the drain there and then."

"He started it!" Dariel snapped. *I think so anyway.*

Athens still had a smugness to his face, surrendering to the shout. "Hey, I wasn't there! Not judging, just saying."

"Well, yes. Dariel, Athens is quite correct, because the comments below were making fun of this man, seriously not buying his story." Godwin finally sat back down. "From what I could find, this man never took his story elsewhere, and thus, the speculation ended with that forum post. No one believed him, I mean, who would? Vampires aren't real, are they? Well," he gestured to himself proudly, "here's a man who chose to believe."

"So you read that and decided I was a suspect?"

Godwin cocked his head and sucked in a breath. "More or less. It could have been a dead end, but I decided to pursue it. I followed your public career from there on, read every article, watched every recording, and I began putting my theories into play. I noted you were never seen out eating, you were never seen in blazing sunshine—though I will add, I know it does not kill you, so that may have just been a preference thing, but I added it to the list nonetheless. You never wear silver jewellery, and you've never publicly had a partner—which again, could all be coincidences, but I gave myself the benefit of the doubt, and they became confirming factors. It would not be fair on your partner if you lived forever, would it?"

Dariel gulped, eyes wide. He felt Athens' arm by his side again, squeezing his bicep in reassurance.

"Impressive how confident you were, Godwin," Athens said.

"My final test was, of course, this evening. I hadn't been able to put my remaining notes into play. I held you outside and you waited until I invited you in before you entered. I placed a secret crucifix in each room, gave you holy water to drink, and I laced your food with garlic, and..."

Athens erupted into laughter. Fully leaning forwards and cradling his stomach.

Dariel sucked in his cheeks to hold his own laughter in. Godwin was so serious as he spoke.

"Have you ever seen *The Lost Boys*? Great movie," Athens said between giggles. "Completely inaccurate but..."

"Well, I..." Godwin began on the defensive, then even his own face dropped into a smile. "Oh, I've been such a buffoon, haven't I?"

"Honestly, the lengths you went to are admirable!" Athens dabbed his eyes.

"The silver, however..." Dariel spoke up, rubbing his fingertips.

"Ah, my apologies, Mr Hale. I honestly didn't believe it would be that bad."

"Doesn't really affect me," Athens added, looking at his nails.

"Well good for you." Dariel wobbled his head sarcastically in Athens' direction, then he noticed all of his silver necklaces had been removed... *How many had he been wearing?*

"So it depends on the vampire, then?" Godwin asked inquisitively.

"I suppose so, haven't really known enough to properly put it to the test," Athens said.

I haven't known any. Dariel thought, but he kept that to himself this time.

"So, gents, please enlighten me where I went wrong. How did you come into being? Were you turned, born this way, what? I wish to know everything." Godwin leaned his elbows onto his knees, ready for answers.

Athens sat up straight. "Hold on, I want to know how I got dragged into this first. I know for definite I've covered my back my entire life."

Dariel admired Athens' confidence in that moment. The other vampire was so sure of himself.

"Ahh, well, Athens dear, you I was always less sure of."

Athens' lip quirked in pride.

'Good.'

'Hey. I said it was an accident. I've been doing this a lot longer than you. It's inevitable.'

'Trust me, darling, I will never slip up.'

'Oh, piss off.'

'No can do. We'll be stuck here for a while now.'

"So what did Athens do to raise your suspicion? He surely made some error somewhere for him to fall onto your radar." Dariel inquired with forced seriousness, leaning forward intently.

'You're a menace.'

'Oh, I'm well aware of that.'

Godwin's face dropped, and Dariel no longer felt like winding anyone up.

"Well, actually, erm. It was a similar thing really. I searched for people who were also in the public eye who seemed to maintain a youthful appearance over a good few years. It was a solid starting point. You're not as publicly known as Dariel, at least your face isn't. Your craft is... well it's magnificent. But after a few false starts with the other people on my radar, I narrowed down to you because well... you did an interview in 2002 that stood out to me."

Athens made no reaction, urging Godwin to continue. "It was in a small magazine. I don't really think many people would have made connections the way I did, but you mentioned something along the lines of being 'reborn' once you started this career five years prior, and I suppose I was just so unhealthily obsessed with finding my answers that the words 'being reborn' as opposed to merely feeling it, was enough for me to speculate. It was simply luck or fate... Something gave me the sense I was on the right lines." Godwin looked ashamed, but he didn't stop. "I ended up down a rabbit hole of more personal connections. You mentioned losing a friend in 1997 in an article. I narrowed down locations and ended up coming across a police report for an accident in a block of flats in early that same year. The flat's owner was pronounced deceased at the scene, and her roommate was missing, presumed dead, but..." Godwin's eyes shot wide as he choked off his words and his hands grabbed for his own neck.

Dariel turned to Athens, the other man sat with a clenched jaw and a face of steel. He could sense the controlling strength leaking from his pores.

Dariel shot out an arm to grip onto Athens' clammy hand, which was glued tightly to his knee.

'Athens, please. Let him go. He means no harm.'

'Does he? Really?'

'You asked him the question!'

Athens began to shake, his breathing rapid. Godwin was still clawing at his neck, trying to find his words.

A tear fell from Athens' face as he let go of Godwin's mind and the other man started panting out breaths, still clutching to his throat.

"I was so careful," Athens muttered, exhausted.

The fire crackled and a roar of hale erupted from the sky outside. The grandfather clock ticked in the distance.

"I was so careful not to..." Athens melted into the sofa, still breathing hard and barely blinking.

"I'm sorry." Godwin finally found his voice again.

Athens wouldn't stop burning his gaze into the human in front of them. As if Godwin, in that moment, held every secret Athens had ever kept in his life.

'Breathe.'

'I...'

'Please. It's okay.' Dariel let his hand wander to Athens' thigh, where he rubbed it gently, warm palms sticking to the vinyl.

"You didn't say anything wrong, Athens. Forgive me. It was all my doing. I was the one who went digging. I couldn't prove it fully... no one else would have gone that far... I..." Godwin sounded panicked.

Athens still didn't speak, though he seemed to have relaxed a little under Dariel's touch.

"I didn't think about what it would be like to—" Godwin was cut off.

"She saved my life... and I... I couldn't save her." Athens finally sat back up straight.

Oh, Athens.

"I'm sorry... I..."

Athens raised a finger to hush their host. "You don't need to apologise... I would have compelled you to tell me anyway. It's my own fault." He sounded like himself again, almost.

They all fell silent once more.

"You don't have to..." Dariel started, not really sure where he wanted the sentence to go, but it was directed at Athens.

Athens waved a hand, brushing him off. "No, I know. What matters is, I got caught! Congratulations Mr Peters, you are officially a vampire hunter!" It wasn't hard to detect the sarcasm in his voice.

Godwin wasn't fazed by this though. Instead, he sat back and dropped his eyelids. "She's looking for you, you know," he said quietly.

"What?" Athens snapped.

It didn't affect Godwin's manner. His hands were trembling in his lap, but his voice did not stutter. "After the accident. You were marked as missing. She's looking for you, your sister. There was a photo of you... only you had a different name... but I knew it was you and..."

She won't miss me. Dariel recalled the other vampire's words from earlier.

Athens gasped in a sharp breath.

Godwin shook his head in sorrow then finally gave in to the confidence he was desperately trying to uphold. "She wants you to be safe."

"No she doesn't." Athens snarled. "She doesn't want *this*." He thumped his fist against his chest, jaw set.

"Athens..." Dariel started, expecting to be pushed away as he reached his arm out again, but instead, Athens leaned down into the embrace and suddenly Dariel found Athens' head in his lap, his fingers beginning to stroke the soft black hair before him.

"Stop now, please," Athens said, like he'd run out of energy.

"Of course, I'm sorry," Godwin said, almost robotically.

"There is a reason the past is the past. It does you no good when you're trying to move forward," Athens continued, his breath warming Dariel's thighs.

'We can leave it where it belongs, everything.'

'I thought I was strong enough.'

'We don't have to unpack anything tonight. Nothing changes my opinion of you, Athens.'

'Thank you.'

Godwin sat with his eyes fixed to the pair of them, their position oddly intimate, Dariel thought. He didn't mind how they looked though, as he continued to smooth Athens' hair down to his shoulders.

"I admire you, Athens. I admire you a great deal. I envy your courage. Your heart," Godwin said.

"Even though it doesn't even beat?" A quiet, subtly joking tone came from Athens then, easing Dariel. He worried perhaps Athens would have grown too far gone into his own mind after that revelation.

Godwin's face softened. "It still beats in your soul, does it not?" He tilted his head to be level with Athens.

Dariel listened to the words as if they were also meant for him, reaching his free hand to his own chest where his heart really did not beat.

He never understood how his body worked. He was dead, but he could bleed. He breathed in air like every other human, but healed wounds at an alarming speed. He wished to learn everything he did not understand from the man still resting his head on his lap. Athens would surely have answers for him. He just needed to keep the pair of them floating above the sea of shadows.

He was not alone, not anymore.

Maybe he didn't have to be again. Even after this night was over.

Rain poured outside, the clock pendulum clicking at a constant pace.

"And you, Dariel Hale. You are wonderful." Godwin smiled.

"I am?" Dariel rubbed his chest. Athens at some point had reached out a hand to stroke his knee, but he only noticed in that moment. *Don't stop.*

"You are my elder, I presume?"

Was that a smirk? Dariel's crotch hardened again. "You really do know us," he said, trying to act unbothered.

'You forget where my head is.'

'No idea what you're talking about.'

'I'm definitely not moving now.'

Dariel discretely pulled a strand of Athens' hair, causing the man in his lap to flinch.

"I believe I am, Mr Peters. I should be retiring." *Fuck it, just flirt. No going back now.*

"Do you remember the war?" Godwin asked sincerely.

"A little. My earliest memory was the end."

Godwin nodded. "Fascinating. Truly, I am... wow. Ha! You're real."

"I suppose I should be thankful I died at the age I did." Dariel asked himself if he'd ever actually felt grateful for that, but the words came naturally. He and Godwin latched onto each other's gazes, and Athens deliberately pressed his head down into Dariel's legs. Heat burned his cheeks—and not from the fire.

"Forever a beauty," Godwin said.

'He's right.'

'You're feeling smug, aren't you?'

'Maybe.'

Dariel might have exploded in that moment. He had run out of flirting techniques—he was, after all, insanely out of practice.

"Okay. What now?" He began, pulling himself away from Athens so the other man had no choice but to sit back up. "You've confirmed your suspicions, we have solidified them for you, so what do you expect from us? We cannot be known. The moment you step out of this house, we will have only one option."

No wonder you've been single this long. Threaten them, that ought to do it.

Godwin clapped his hands together, mellowing. "Well. That will be no problem, dear Dariel. For I summoned you both here this evening to..." he took in a deep breath, eyes glassy. "Well, to kill me."

"I'm sorry?" Athens shouted, causing Dariel to jump. In the last five minutes of having Athens purely in his head, he'd already forgotten how loud the man could be.

Godwin beamed, but his hands trembled even more so than before. His body was betraying him. "You heard me right. Though after the evening we've all had, I'm sure that has now come as quite a shock."

"I'm not going to kill you," Dariel blurted out, confident in his statement. He would not raise a finger to this man. No. Never. He'd killed once before and refused to even come close to doing it again.

"You have no choice, though, do you?" Godwin said.

"We would simply erase your memory of the evening," Athens said, indicating he was on the same page as Dariel. "No harm will come to you, I promise."

"Ah, but then you'd have to erase the last decade of my life. I'd rather die with the knowledge than go on as a man without his mind."

Neither of them spoke.

"I never expected you both to answer my invitation, but you did. Now my wish is one step closer to coming true."

Dariel weighed the options the moment Godwin revealed his knowledge. Either they wiped all memory of their existence from his mind, or they stopped him from ever speaking to another human for the rest of his life. Though it seemed he was doing a fine job of the latter himself anyway, Dariel had been too entranced by this man to ever let his mind wander to any other option. To the very idea Godwin may have to die. A human man had found not one, but two vampires; creatures the world really did not know existed—not in any believable state. He could not live on with this knowledge, and simply wiping his memory may do more damage than good. But murder? No. Dariel couldn't.

"Godwin, I know what we said, but we really do not want to have to do this. Let us cause you to forget us. It is the easiest option for us all. No one has to be harmed," Dariel tried, still worrying even this option may not work. He could sense the rising pulse of their host; noting the beads of sweat on his forehead.

"I don't want to forget you," Godwin said, his voice innocent and childlike. His terror was plain to see.

"Godwin... I..." *I don't want to make you forget us.*

"Why?" Athens cried. "Why do you want to die?"

Godwin wiped his eyes. "It is simply my wish. I decided a while ago I wanted my life to end, that I was coming to the end of my time on this earth, but I..."

"WHY? Why is your life not worth living? And why go to the extremes of finding *vampires* to do it?" Athens was speaking so loud now, his voice shaking in time with Godwin's hands.

Their host's breathing grew erratic as he raised a trembling hand to his face, covering his mouth.

"Godwin? Why? Please. I don't want to do this," Dariel pleaded.

"I didn't think I'd grow so fond of you both this quickly. One evening should never have the effect this one has had on one's opinion of strangers but…" he choked up. "I do rather like you both."

"So let us help! After everything you shared with us, we cannot let you *die*. You haven't even let yourself live yet! You've been cooped up in this *prison* for far too long. You're mortal. Time is precious. And you wasted a whole lot of it." *Why are you crying now Dariel? Pull yourself together.*

"Oh, Dariel. You really are a bonny man, inside and out. I am glad I found you."

"Shut up! It doesn't matter what you say or think about me. This is about *you*. We will not let you die!" Dariel hadn't realised he was standing until he felt a soft hand reach out to pull him back. Athens.

"Godwin. You are not going anywhere. Your soul is staying put," the other man said harshly.

"I made my decision." Godwin was not budging.

"Well you'll have to find someone else to do it, because we're wiping your memories then we're leaving." It was Athens' turn to stand. He walked over to Godwin and bent down to his eye level.

"What! NO! I want to die *with* my memories. I want this evening to be just as it was. The moments we shared, the wisdom the both of you gave me. You helped me *see* and understand I am not alone!"

'If we helped him, why does he still want to die? I don't understand.'

'Sometimes these things run a lot deeper. He's a stubborn man. Reminds me of myself.'

'You wanted to die?'

'Not exactly.'

'Athens?'

'I'm still here, aren't I?' Athens still crouched in front of Godwin, arms rooted to each side of the sofa, locking their host in.

"Don't," Dariel said out loud. Though he wasn't sure who he was talking to. *Don't take his memories. Don't leave me. Don't.*

"Fine." Athens stood up abruptly, dusting off his hands but still towering over Godwin on the Chesterfield.

Dariel heard Godwin's audible sigh of relief, despite the remaining tension in the room.

"You're so sure you want to die, fine. I will kill you."

'What? No! I won't let you…'

'Relax. I'm not going to kill him.'

'You're not?'

'I'm only letting him believe it.'

'Why? I don't understand.'

'You fancy sticking around for a little longer than one night?'

'What? Well I…'

Yes. Yes I do.

"I will kill you, Godwin Peters, but not yet. You're going to tell us how you hoped the rest of the evening would play out first."

Athens finally moved out of the way to let the other man stand. Godwin lowered his head in thanks to Athens.

"How did you envision leaving this world?" Athens kept his tone sharp.

Godwin cowered a little. "Oh, well, it feels stupid to say it out loud finally, and I made assumptions I perhaps shouldn't have, but…"

"Nothing is stupid. Not tonight. What do you want?"

"I want it to be pleasant. I want my dying moments to be blissful, to make me *feel,* and I want my last breath to be one of relief. I have lived this life, it was set out for me, but now it is time to leave. I do not wish to grow old, ha." Godwin swallowed and closed his eyes with a ghost of a smile across his lips. "I want one last moment to remember what I once had." He sighed as if it were already his last breath, pausing before he finished and dipping his head once more. "It is pathetic really, and only attests to the selfishness that has always lain within me—this lust—but it is what I wish for."

Dariel scowled. Then his face softened.

'Did you hear that?'

'I...huh.'

"Well, Godwin Peters," Athens patted him on the back, "If you're asking a man into your bed, you could at least show him your record collection first."

Chapter Nine

Dariel didn't know how to feel. He'd gone through every emotion he had the ability to experience in such a short space of time, and it made him rather nauseous.

Godwin led the way upstairs, nodding to himself. Athens turned back to Dariel with a tongue-in-cheek side eye.

It was clear now why the upstairs had been out of bounds.

Godwin hadn't wanted them to know his plan yet. He'd wanted to get to know them both before he asked them what he just did.

The bedroom.

When Godwin's confession emerged, Dariel was immediately shocked—then *intrigued*. He wanted to die, which hurt Dariel a great deal, but before his death, he desired a bed partner. One final time. *To die with relief.*

The thought sent blood rushing to Dariel's cheeks—the constant anatomical marvel he would never understand.

He shook the question away, not wanting to dwell on the sensations the thought of being in Godwin's bed with the man by his side, *on top of him,* made him feel. He focused on Godwin's back up the stairs: the way he slightly favoured his right side, the ruffle of his shirt under the superbly fitted waist coat, and the multitude of colours woven into his hair—all silver and gold and sun-spun silk.

Stop it, Dariel. He said it himself! He had not expected you both. It was Athens who promised to grant his wish. You will be on your way soon. No longer needed.

But the very idea of the slender, leather clad, obsidian dream of a man taking Godwin to bed alone was torture. And Dariel didn't quite know who he was more jealous of.

He noted the hot peach flush to Godwin's cheeks as he turned to the top of the stairs, then his eyes lowered to the banister, and to the onyx, slightly pointed nails on each now ringless finger of Athens' hand.

You really must stop this, Dariel. It will do you no good.

'What are you thinking, darling?'

Dariel stopped dead, three steps from the top, the other two men staring down, waiting for him.

'Oh, I... I'm not quite sure.'

'Your mind seemed occupied. Do not worry, I have this whole evening under control.'

Dariel attempted to smile, nodding his head subtly as he reached the top.

Athens raised his arm out to clap a hand on Dariel's back, which made him shudder.

Don't tease me, please. Though how could he forget the way Athens had spoken to him earlier? Had that all been a ruse? Or did Athens really still like him? *You only met this evening.*

It confused him, and the past half an hour had done nothing to help ease his mind in any way.

"It's err, right this way, gents," Godwin said with his hands on his hips. If he noticed any intimacy to the patting gesture, he did not show it. He guided the pair of them towards a far door—one they hadn't gotten around to trying earlier.

Godwin produced a bunch of keys from his pocket—quite a

large bunch they were—and unlocked the door to reveal a relatively small room in comparison to most others they'd seen. It was still larger than any spare room Dariel had owned though, even in his richest days.

It was a cold, cream painted room that smelled slightly foisty, with the two sash windows on the far wall sealed shut with glossy white paint. In one corner stood a green velvet chaise lounge, rimmed in ornate brass, and behind it was a wall of built-in shelves with glass doors. On the right wall closest to the door stood a relatively retro record player, but far more modern than Dariel expected. Something that may have been state of the art some thirty years ago, but now a worn and slightly dented sign of the times. Two large speakers were bolted to the wall above it, the metal supports having been painted over a number of times to be concealed. The floor was covered in a deep green carpet, which was notably thread bare in some patches. This struck Dariel as a once loved room, but one that had not been touched in a number of years. A collection of framed posters were stacked in the corner, the front showing a deep blue image of someone swimming—

"Oh, cool! Siouxsie and the Banshees!" Athens dove over to the pictures, dropping to his knees immediately and pulling the frame out with both hands to admire, dusting it off. Godwin walked over behind him with a small gruff of a chuckle, hands back on his hips.

"Ah, yes. I told you I was quite a fan of that stuff once. Late seventies, early eighties... I used to allow myself some joys," he said.

Athens turned to him, looking up with pleading, puppy dog eyes, not allowing Godwin to dwell. "You need to show me your collection, right now."

Dariel decided to step over to join them, otherwise he would very quickly begin to feel left out. He watched as Godwin opened the cabinets to reveal boxes and boxes filled with 12-inch records, pulling out the closest one and dusting the decades of dust from the lid before opening it.

Athens sneezed into his elbow then began rummaging eagerly.

Dariel swallowed. He was much more of a nineties man, never cared for eighties music as much as he would have liked, despite spending most of that decade in America, surrounded by the stuff. He spent most of the early nineties, before his career really kicked off, dancing from club-to-club with dance anthem after dance anthem, bouncing around until the drink knocked him out, or he simply ran out of breath. Quite a time to remember.

He hadn't noticed Godwin had turned to face him. "What sort of music do you like, Dariel?" he asked, green eyes glinting.

Athens' head was deep inside the cupboard.

"Oh, well. A bit of everything, I suppose. I lost a lot of time for music once my work took over."

"A shame. We have both been robbed of our joys then," Godwin asserted, which Dariel knew was intended as a joke, but it still struck him as odd. Both of them had plenty of free rein over whether they chose to listen to music or not. Dariel couldn't find the time, Godwin didn't *want* to.

"A classic!" Athens broke the moment by pulling out a plastic-coated LP and holding it up like the body of Christ in Communion.

Dariel didn't recognise the gold cover. Godwin took a moment to take it in before his face changed. "Oh, my. A throwback indeed, if only I had a working player. The radio truly does disappoint these days."

Athens smirked. "Oh, my dear Godwin, let me introduce you to the iPod. Give me a second..." he carefully replaced the LP then ran out of the door. Dariel heard the distant heavy stomps of his feet hurry down the stairs. He breathed out into the sudden silence, losing his voice momentarily.

"He's a sprightly fellow now, isn't he?" Godwin stood, shaking his head. Then he looked head on at Dariel. "Must be nice looking at everyone your real age knowing you'll never grow old. I've not been able to run that fast in donkey's years."

Dariel kept his face blank. "Growing old is natural," he said.

"You're right, but still," Godwin stepped closer, "it must be freeing."

"Maybe sometimes. It's not as magical as it sounds though. I worry..." Dariel swallowed, "I worry one day I will begin to forget my earliest memories, like a child can't remember learning to walk, but instead I'll forget I was ever human at all. The time will come when this will be all I know."

Before Godwin could respond, Athens ran back into the room holding the latest MP3 with earphones, wheezing. "Here... look..." he said, unwinding the wires from the device.

"I... I do know what an iPod is, I'm not a true hermit. I have the internet." Godwin sounded mildly offended, but kept his tone light. He briefly glanced at Dariel, acknowledgement from their unfinished conversation in his eyes, before looking down at the player in Athens' hands.

"Ahh, you don't own one though, do you? You do not understand the excitement of being able to download 80GB of songs... Do you know how many songs that could be? All within the push of a button? It's truly ingenious. Here... I have the perfect song." Athens reached over to Godwin with one earbud in hand, the other already in his own ear. Dariel took a step back. Neither of them looked at him now, at least not while he took in the sight of them both beginning to smile and nod their heads to the beat of the tune. One Dariel couldn't hear.

Perhaps this was truly where his own evening should end. He should call a cab home, or at least ask to retire to one of the bedrooms alone. Athens seemed perfectly capable of handling the rest of the evening without him, had even expressed so... it would be fine if he just...

"Here, Dariel, listen. You can't *not* enjoy this song!" Athens had pulled out his own earbud and was dangling the wire in Dariel's direction.

Oh.

He accepted, stepping over and taking Athens' place, turning to Godwin as the music commenced.

Oh.

"Good, no? The sound quality is insane." Athens was beaming, black-lined eyes wide as he nodded along to the tune he couldn't even hear anymore.

'You can borrow it whenever you like.'

Dariel sharply turned his head to Athens, the bud falling out and dangling on the wire. His brow tensed.

'You...'

Athens folded his arms; Godwin retrieved the other bud and enjoyed the music to the fullest.

'You can tell me what stuff you like, maybe I can broaden my horizons.'

'You want to spend more time with me still?'

'Is that truly such a shock to you?'

'But I thought... what you said to Godwin...'

"Athens! A gem! You've reawakened something in me, ha!" Godwin shouted loudly over the music in his ears. He was shuffling his feet in the slightest effort of a dance.

"You like?" Athens asked, reaching over to Godwin and adjusting the earphones in his ears, their skin touching as he did so, Dariel noticed. The pair locked eyes for a moment which caused Dariel's stomach to sink.

Why couldn't he understand what was going on?

"This really takes me back. Ha! I'm in my early thirties again. I've not heard this song since..." Godwin's face dropped slightly.

Athens wasted no time in preventing the negative dwelling again. "I've got a list of bands you must listen to, very similar vibes, but all doing something new and unique. There's a record shop not too far from here I don't think. We should go some time, after I get my friend to fix your player of course, which..." Athens wandered over to the record player and inspected the make and model, flicking his eyes over parts and playing around with the tonearm, likely trying to figure out the issue, "should be an easy fix. I'll get my mate to take a look…"

Finally, Dariel understood. This was all part of Athens' plan. He never intended on killing Godwin. Only to show him how worth life could be living, even if it was just the small things.

Godwin didn't seem to acknowledge what Athens had implied. That he would be here past this evening. He was still clutching onto the iPod with a smile across his face, mind wandering.

Huh.

Their next endeavour of the evening was the wardrobe *room*. Athens insisted the three of them had a look around, calling it a fun exercise in learning more about Godwin whilst it also being 'a fashion designer's dream'—he glared at Dariel as he said the last part.

Godwin unlocked another door further up the landing and Dariel's first thought was one of relief—that this room actually did seem used. Lived in. Not quite the shrine of halcyon days the record room had been.

If the original plan had turned out to be real, Dariel thought he would have rather enjoyed coming up with a new wardrobe for his host. Godwin already had style—a rather attractive one too— all beiges and browns. Green braces, waistcoat, and corduroy trousers—the post-war look Dariel grew up around. It was oddly comforting to see an entire wardrobe full of the clothes of his time as a human. Hangers of well-worn and appreciated items, not stuck in the back of an antique shop or on display in educational visitors' sites. Without even thinking, Dariel traced his fingers over the shirts in the mahogany wardrobe closest to him, flitting his gaze to the hat boxes and polished shoes at the foot of the cupboard. His chest fluttered.

"I'm quite... different to you both, as you can see. I never enjoyed the lavish life of experimenting with accessories and such, though I wish I had." Godwin had positioned himself on the stool beside the dressing table in the far corner. The light buzzed above them.

"Nonsense. I adore vintage," Athens said, hands in the pockets of his low-rise trousers. Dariel caught the briefest glimpse of skin where the other man's top had risen slightly, the material hugging his waist, defining the slight curve of his hips. Dariel quickly snapped his gaze back to the clothes in front of him, teeth biting into his lip. Athens wandered over to the single window and began looking out into the evening rain. It was growing quite late, though Dariel hadn't checked the time for quite a while. He continued to rummage.

Then he saw them. Right at the back of the wardrobe.

"Oh, Godwin!" Dariel beamed, carefully pulling out the polished brown brogues he'd found, holding the soles with care. "I used to have a pair exactly like these!"

"You did?" Godwin shot up and walked over to get a closer look. "Oh, I used to love those shoes. Early sixties I think, they were my fathers." His voice was ever so slightly bitter at the mention of his family, though it seemed his thoughts were growing far beyond that now. "Try them on! What size are you?"

They should be the right size.

Dariel jumped over to the cushioned bench against the window and began to try them on. They wouldn't fit his attire at all, in fact looked rather silly, but joy flooded his senses as memories came flooding back...

Annette.

Dariel gulped, a lump forming deep in his throat. He looked down at the brogues on his feet, dizziness whirling around him like a storm.

"My wife got me these... as a wedding present," he heard himself say. "I lost them in the... there was a fire."

"Oh, oh, Dariel." It was Godwin's sympathy he heard first, the human stepping over and bending to his knees in front of him. "Forgive me, if I'd known..."

Instead of letting the memories consume him though, he frowned. "Whatever do you have to be sorry for? I pulled them out, I wanted to remember... They made me happy."

'We can change rooms if you'd rather, darling?'

Dariel swallowed hard again and looked up to where Athens stood, both men positioned rather close to him now, modelled in expressions of melancholy.

Darling. He said it again. And again. He keeps saying it.

"I'm okay, honestly," Dariel said aloud, lifting his legs to admire the shoes. "But who am I kidding? I'm only a size seven." They all laughed.

They continued to look about; Athens pulling out what were, in his words, the more 'out there' items, and instructed Godwin on how best to style a bow tie. Godwin produced his selection of full-length ties and Dariel went to town on picking out the ones he liked the most, holding them up to Godwin from a distance, squinting and focusing on what would suit the man best.

"I think red suits you quite well, you know," Dariel announced. "You should try incorporating a few pops of colour. This red tie perhaps, or even red socks." He imagined Godwin in a soft pair of red socks under his beige trousers and wondered if that was what Victorian men would feel when they caught a glimpse of their wives' ankles.

"I always wished to own a burgundy shirt. Though I never found one I liked in shops," Godwin said, casting his mind back.

"Well then, I'm sure Dariel can fix you up with something. He'll know all the best places in London, isn't that right?" Athens moved to join Godwin's side, but he looked at Dariel. Again, working his subtle magic.

"Oh, of course. I know the places to look where most other people don't bother." Dariel joined in, noting the delighted expression on Godwin's face.

"Speaking of shirts!" Godwin leaped up, both knees clicking as he stood. "I just remembered something... bear with me!"

He wandered to the opposite side of the room and opened a wardrobe Dariel hadn't gotten around to yet.

Athens made himself busy in the dressing table drawers, long hair trailing over the tabletop.

Godwin started humming to himself as he raked through the shirts and Dariel noted it was the same song he'd been listening to in the other room.

"Ahh, ha!" Godwin produced a sheer black shirt with large, ruffled sleeves and a deep V-neck collar. It looked like something fresh from the clothing trunk of a pirate boat, or perhaps a medieval forest gathering. Dariel had these specific images in his head, which was to say, it was a cool shirt.

"I can picture you in this, Dariel!" Godwin said, making Dariel freeze with the words. *He can picture me wearing a sheer shirt?* His breathing went funny.

"With a few more layers, of course," the words left Dariel's mouth before he could catch them.

Godwin's heart fluttered and... he blushed. "Of course," he said, though he turned his head to the floor as he spoke, clearing his throat.

Maybe he could take it off me.

Honestly, Dariel. You're disappointing every version of yourself here.

"This was Gareth's," Godwin announced. *His old partner,* Dariel surmised. The arousal he'd felt mere seconds ago instantly fizzled with a pop in his mind.

"Oh, well I wouldn't want to..."

"Nonsense! He gave it to me. Though I never had the confidence to wear it. Here..." Godwin stepped up close to Dariel, breath kissing his skin as he held the shirt up to Dariel and his knuckles brushed Dariel's cheek.

Oh, God. Heat rushed all over Dariel's body, his legs threatening to give way. He was too close, he wouldn't be able to contain himself for much longer if Godwin kept looking at him that way and...

'Come here, darling.'

Athens was behind Dariel in an instant, though Godwin barely stepped back, only lowering the shirt slightly. Dariel watched Godwin watching as Athens produced a string of small pearls and fastened them around Dariel's neck—his breath hot on the skin below his ear as he brushed away Dariel's hair to clasp it shut.

"Now who's a pretty boy?" Athens said in a comical tone, but it was enough to send Dariel's thoughts to only one thing as Athens prowled around to see his work, both hands scooped under the shirt collar onto Dariel's bare shoulders. *No rings.*

Godwin held up a hand, his face blank. "Oh, those were my..." he shook his head, "Oh, what the hell, you wear them better than she ever did." He leaned forward and squeezed Dariel's biceps, admiring him wholly. Athens hadn't let go of him yet.

They were both touching him.

He could sense the pounding of Godwin's pulse, the rush of heat over the other man's body.

Oh, fuck.

'You're very attractive when you do that, you know.'

'Do what?'

'You're breathing fast through your nose, you're trying to restrain yourself, but you're not doing a very good job.'

Godwin pulled back at the exact same time Athens did, and though it was pure coincidence, Dariel saw it as a tease. The body heat of the other two disappeared instantaneously whilst Dariel had to cling onto every last ounce of self-restraint he had before he combusted.

"I... erm..." Dariel thought it was himself speaking, but it was actually Godwin. He stepped away and hung the shirt on the handles of the now closed wardrobe door, rubbing his palms down his trousers.

"A question," Athens said rather abruptly. Dariel turned to him, trying to read his face.

Athens clasped his hands together. "I believe it is getting rather late, don't you?"

"Oh, well, yes. Maybe," Godwin grew flustered, looking around as if he'd lost time in the boxes and clothes around him.

"Don't worry, the night is still young, but my question is a rather important one."

Godwin raised his head high to indicate he was listening.

Athens stepped over to Dariel's side, clearly displaying the easy five or six inches between them. Dariel's eyes wandered all the way up and down Athens' body, ears burning.

Athens' hand found his, and as the warm, slender fingers wrapped around his skin, he finally realised Athens had taken every ounce of his jewellery off. Earrings, the lot. *Did he do that all for me?*

Dariel's stomach flipped.

"Of course, your wish was to take one of us to bed with you. I believe we concluded I would be filling the role of bed partner this evening, though it hardly seems fair to leave such a handsome fellow out, now does it?" Athens said.

Godwin was a deer in headlights. "Oh, well I..." he rubbed his hands against his trousers again, clearing his throat for the thousandth time. "I was rather hoping you both could join me this evening... if that's what you'd both be comfortable with?"

Oh, God.

'Would you be comfortable with that?'
'I thought you'd never ask.'

"I would like that. A lot." Dariel thought it good measure to verbalise his consent.

"Excellent, then lead the way to the bedroom, Godwin, dear," Athens said, pointing to the door with his free hand, his other having tightened on Dariel's own.

Godwin didn't move though. "Oh, well. I quite wish to erm... It's been a very long while, you see, and I'd quite like to freshen up and... prepare." He looked to the side of Dariel, heart pounding again.

'Oh, this is going to be a lot of fun.'

Godwin produced a key. "It's erm, the room on the..."

"We know which room, dear," Athens cooed.

Godwin nodded frantically, mumbling then handing the brass key to Dariel as Athens turned to face him.

"Well then, we'll go and get a head start, won't we darling?"

Chapter Ten

The last time Dariel had let anyone into his bed was about seven years prior. It was the dawn of a new millennium, and he'd been invited to a gala of some sorts, he didn't really remember what it was for. His agent would secure all the events and all he had to do was turn up and look pretty in something he'd designed. They were showing off a few of his pieces at some point during the evening and would be auctioning something off to charity. It was a free bar though, so once the exchanging of pleasantries had ended, he decided it was time to unwind. An hour after the clock struck midnight, he stumbled home with a pretty thirty-two-year-old woman who knew exactly what she liked in bed. He was her 'pretty prince' for three months before he realised he really could not do relationships... not while he was Dariel Hale, one of the most known alternative British designers of the late nineties. Too much press, too much hiding. He liked to keep life as simple as it could be. He didn't enjoy lying.

But now? He was free. No strings, no expectations, just a choice to make the evening as pleasurable as possible for Godwin. A job role Dariel very much wanted to take on.

Godwin wandered off to shower as Athens took Dariel back down towards the room.

The room. The ornate bed with gold trimmings and eccentric wallpaper with three pillows set across the bed. Dariel hadn't homed in on that detail when he'd first looked through the keyhole, though it was at the forefront of his mind now that he realised Godwin had expected them both to say yes all along.

Athens worked the key into the lock as Dariel stood watching, trying to manage his breathing.

"You took your jewellery off," he said matter-of-factly.

Athens winked as he pushed the door wide open. "Of course I did, I knew I'd have to before I touched you."

Hands all over your body.

Holding you.

Kissing you.

"Just get inside," Dariel demanded, his eyelids feeling heavy. He couldn't take this any longer.

Athens served a hungry grin. "Oh, so demanding." Then he pulled Dariel into the room with him and slammed the door behind them, pushing Dariel up against it, hand clasping his shirt front.

Dariel had a handful of seconds to process the room was lit by a dim, golden chandelier and a collection of fake candles dotted around before Athens' breath was on his skin, his lips so close to pressing to his neck.

"You're such a tease, you know that?" Athens breathed into Dariel's ear, pulling their bodies together.

Dariel rolled into the pressure against his chest, back arching off the door slightly. "*I'm* a tease?" His brow quirked up.

Athens stood back to take in Dariel's whole body as if he was a canvas on display, before lifting his hands to delicately unclasp all the necklaces around Dariel's neck in silence. Dariel savoured the touch, closing his eyes and letting himself relax. Once his neck was bare, Athens moved away and placed the pearls and thin chains gently on the cabinet beside them.

"You, coming in and looking at me with those bright blue eyes, hair styled like that, tight high waisted trousers leaving very little to the imagination." Athens' eyes flitted down to Dariel's crotch, causing Dariel's cheeks to heat up and he instinctively threw a hand in front of himself.

"They fit perfectly fine when I left the house." He gulped, eyes blazing into Athens'.

"Unbutton your shirt," Athens said, cocking his head slightly as if he were still inspecting Dariel like a Greek statue in the centre of a gallery.

Dariel did as he was told, fingers fumbling down the buttons as Athens stepped forward, hunger and desire raging in his glacier eyes. The taller man pressed their heads together as Dariel looked up through his lashes.

"Nah, ah! Not all the way." Athens grabbed at where Dariel's hands were halfway down the shirt, clasping them tightly, pulling them away from the fabric and slowly lowering them. Athens reached an arm out to cup Dariel's neck; their foreheads parting slightly as the pair of them panted into each other's mouths.

"Don't untuck it yet, I want to push it over... there..." Athens whispered, brushing Dariel's half open shirt over his shoulders so the skin of his chest and the tops of his arms were fully exposed beneath Athens' gaze. Goosebumps ran over his flesh as Athens leaned down to hungrily kiss his neck and Dariel fully melted into the sensation, letting Athens hold him up. A strained moan escaped his lips as Athens licked and sucked; letting his full, berry lips trace the skin across Dariel's collar bone, pressing in hard at the hollow of his throat where the clavicles met. Dariel tipped his head back in fevered ecstasy, resting the back of his skull against the door frame as Athens wrapped an arm under his shirt, encircling his bare back. The contrast of warm and cold sent a chill of pleasure down his spine as the other man pulled their bodies close, right arm around his neck, holding his head up with fingers curling tightly into the white-blond waves at the base of Dariel's head.

'Kiss me.'

'I am, darling.' Athens' mouth had continued to wander across the top of Dariel's chest.

'My lips. Eat my lips.'

"Gladly," Athens said, looking into Dariel's eyes, pupils blown wide, lips parting as he breathed heavily before devouring Dariel's mouth entirely.

Teeth and tongues clashed and locked, Athens pulling Dariel tighter to his chest as Dariel wrapped both arms around Athens' neck and they were rocking together, Dariel's shirt naturally coming untucked from his trousers as they melted their bodies into one, every perfect shape of Athens' body slotting into Dariel's.

Neither of them wanted to unstitch their arms from each other, so Dariel did his best to shrug his shirt further down his arms until he could let it pool around the crooks of his elbows and his waist, cold air hitting his back as he did so. Athens' warm hands had already started tracing the lines of his shoulder-blades before he even had a chance to feel any discomfort.

'I'm so hungry.'

'I've been starved for too long.'

They stumbled forwards as Dariel forced more weight into the connection, a mass of stolen breaths and un-beating hearts. Dariel combed his fingers up through Athens' silky black and red hair, digging his nails around the roots, their lips still locked.

'The best meal I've had in a while.' Athens swallowed one last breath from Dariel before letting his mouth roam back down pale skin, Dariel tipping his head back and arching backwards over Athens' arm that still held him close, fingers pressing into Athens' shoulders as he let out a cry.

Dariel shuddered under the touch, forcing his weight forward even more to press Athens into the chest of drawers behind them, wobbling them slightly and knocking something from the top. He could feel the quirk of Athens' mouth against his skin as he pushed back.

'Careful there, darling, we don't want to wreck the place now, do we?'

Dariel couldn't think, he was miles away in some sea of midnight silk. Eyes dreary, lungs empty.

"Touch me, touch me, touch me. Hold me, Athens," he panted out his pleas. Athens grumbled a laugh from the back of his throat as he worked his way down to the waistband of Dariel's trousers, undoing the rest of the shirt buttons, allowing Dariel to fully escape from the fabric and throwing it to the floor out of the way.

Athens was on one knee for a moment, looking up with both his fingers wrapped around Dariel's waist. His eyes watching the in and out breaths frantically escaping Dariel's chest.

"Beautiful," Athens said, batting his lashes and sucking in his lip, letting a lengthened canine pull away the skin a bit. A dribble of blood trickled down his chin.

"Oh," Dariel gasped as he crumbled to his knees in front of Athens and caught the trail with his tongue, pushing it into a kiss and cupping both of Athens' cheeks feverishly.

'When was the last time you fed?' Athens whispered in their minds as he held Dariel as though he was made of glass, thumbs lightly tracing his nipples.

'I, erm... earlier. The taxi...' "Ugh." Dariel couldn't contain himself, the sounds that escaped his mouth he forgot he had the capability of making as they rocked into each other once more.

'Oh, poor driver.' Athens joked, beginning to lean over Dariel, lowering them to the ground beside the bed like dance partners; slowly pressing Dariel into the faux fur rug beneath them.

'I was tempted.' Dariel let his bent legs stretch out to either side of Athens as he was lowered fully onto the rug, the soft fluff tickling his back. Athens caged over him with his arms to either side

and he bent down to kiss Dariel's neck, long hair sliding over his shoulders, covering his face, and brushing over Dariel's skin.

"You are exquisite," Athens said between kisses down Dariel's body. Dariel arched his spine again to savour the touch of Athens' lips against his skin. He let out a gasp as Athens' teeth found his left nipple and *pulled.*

"Wait until he joins us, he will devour you and I'm going to have to keep some for myself," Athens said, rolling his body back up to nibble at Dariel's ear.

Oh, God, Godwin too.

Athens ground his hips into Dariel's, gasping for a full breath. "He's preparing himself for *you,*" he said, reaching a hand between them and rubbing a flat palm over Dariel's erection. Dariel's eyes rolled back in his head, picturing not only Athens' hands doing that, but Godwin's too.

Oh, fuck.

"Athens," he breathed out, all restraint leaving his throat. Athens pressed his palm down harder and curled his fingers around the shape beneath Dariel's trousers, hovering his head above Dariel's; hair fringing Dariel's view so he could only see Athens' face.

"That's it, darling. Say my name."

"Athens. Oh, Athens, I... *ahh.*"

'I enjoy seeing you like this.' Athens brushed the hair from Dariel's now damp forehead, making a feigned sad face. "Oh dear, I'm ruining your makeup."

Dariel swallowed, his throat bobbing as he gagged out another breath, his hands now flopped above his head in surrender.

"I want..." Dariel started.

"What do you want, my dear?" Athens teased his fingers under the rim of Dariel's waistband, eliciting a squirm and squeal.

After a further few minutes of hot breaths and aching moans, Dariel finally managed to find an ounce of strength and pushed himself up onto his elbows, Athens drawing back to a sitting position.

"You first," Dariel pointed to Athens' layered top, one of the straps having come loose at some point as they lost themselves in each other's arms. "Take this off."

There was a brief moment of silence as Athens straightened out his back and flicked his long mane of hair over his shoulders, pressing his own hand to his chest. Dariel frantically searched for the best place to stare to stop himself from shattering completely, his hips still locked between the taller man's thighs. Athens watched him looking and maintained eye contact as he reached for the zip to the side of his over-top, peeling the bodice away from his body slowly, letting the buckled straps slide off until all that was left was a thin, black mesh top. Dariel sat up, sliding himself out from under, and drank in the other man's form. The curve of his hips, the long slender neck leading up to bruised lips and black-rimmed, marble eyes. A few strands of hair stuck to Athens' pale forehead and Dariel thought *huh, I did that* before grinning.

"And the rest," he nodded towards the mesh still holding Athens' body away from him, begging to have their bodies pressed together again.

'So impatient!' Athens closed his eyes with a sensual laugh and pulled the remaining top over his shoulders, throwing it to the growing pile of clothes beside them. His bare torso was free at last, finally exposing the interconnecting black and white rose petal tattoos that wove around Athens' left arm like vines—confirming Dariel's suspicions. *Pretty.*

Dariel's eyes widened slightly. "Oh, you're..." he raised a gentle hand to ghost his fingers over the two horizontal scars across the centre of Athens' chest.

The other man swallowed as he followed Dariel's movement. "Trans, yes. I should have..."

"God, no." Dariel gasped out a breath of joy. "You're so hot." He leaned up on his knees and kissed the centre of Athens' chest, holding the other man by his shoulder blades, hands splayed out and exploring Athens' back as he let his own lips wander this time.

"Not a problem, then?" Athens tilted his head down to kiss Dariel's crown, both hands on his head, fingers knitting into the bleached curls.

"No. God, no," Dariel said between kisses, fully focused on exploring every inch of skin in front of him.

"Good. I'm gonna...ugh... stand and..." Athens pried himself away from Dariel's grip and stood, leaving a very hungry vampire at his feet, arms still out, pleading for Athens' warmth. Dariel began to raise to his feet but was halted by a long finger to the face.

"Stay on your pretty knees, darling."

'Oh, you wanna play this game?'

'Do you mind?'

'Not at all.'

Dariel shuffled over to be eye level with Athens' hips, the sticky vinyl in front of him teasing his hunger. Athens moved into the embrace of Dariel's arms again, letting Dariel grasp at Athens' behind, drawing them even closer together with a jolt. He almost knocked Athens off his feet. Athens steadied himself on Dariel's shoulders as Dariel moved his hands around to worship the other man's thighs.

"I'm gonna take my shoes off so you can..."

"Oh, please. I need..."

"What do you need?" Athens teased, looking down at Dariel who still hugged his left thigh. He dropped the pointed nail of this thumb onto Dariel's lower lip, pressing down. "Tell me what you need."

'You know what I need.'

'Let me get these off.'

In a matter of seconds, Athens and Dariel were both barefoot, the top button of Athens' trousers undone, and Dariel's shaking fingers slowly pulled down the shallow zip to allow himself to peel the trousers off as slowly as he desired, Athens watching him all the way.

Once they too had been discarded, Dariel arched up to tug at the lace of Athens' underwear with his teeth and tore them down the trembling thighs he still held in his grip, until the man before him was entirely naked. Athens gasped, throwing his head back, fingers biting into Dariel's neck.

Dariel paced himself as much as he could, savouring the taste of the other man's groin and hip bones, moving his hands back to squeeze Athens' ass as he dragged his tongue along the sensitive skin of each side of Athens' inner thighs. A fine dusting of fair hair trailed up to Athens' belly button, dancing over the soft skin of his lower abdomen.

"I'm trying so hard not to rush... I don't want..." Dariel swallowed, "I don't want this to end."

"Good thing this is just the beginning then. Do whatever you like, I am yours."

I am yours. Dariel thought he may pass out.

"Can I?" Dariel gazed all the way up to Athens's face in sheer desperation.

Athens grinned, lifting Dariel's chin, and swallowing hard. "I'm sure you know how to pleasure a man like me?"

Dariel nodded eagerly, tipping his chin out as his free thumb reached up to circle Athens' clit, the man in his arms crying out, his legs shaking beneath Dariel's grip.

"Spread your legs for me, will you?" Dariel asked, though Athens had already moved into position before he could finish, allowing Dariel to reach up and continue the movement with the flick of his tongue, dragging it up and down the lips, listening for the cries of pleasure erupting from Athens' mouth.

I'm doing that, as well, he thought.

Dariel let his tongue roam, Athens clenching and loosening around him, and he let his mind wander to Godwin, imagining the larger man standing behind him and stroking his warm hands up and down Dariel's arms as he continued to drink from Athens.

'Are you thinking about him?'

'How could you tell?'

'I am too. He won't be much longer... We should...woah Dariel, you really do know how to...' Athens let out a moan.

'Oh that sound does things to me, you have no idea.' Dariel sped up for good measure.

"Holy shit," Athens cried out, nails almost drawing blood on the skin of Dariel's back before his legs gave way entirely, and Dariel had to slow the fall with his hands.

Now Athens sat before him with his knees bent, legs hiked up, glistening cunt on full display. Dariel crawled over to him, eyes locking again as fingers reached to circle the entrance.

"I want you inside me," Athens panted as their brows collided. He grasped Dariel's head. "We need to... get you out of those." Athens knocked a knee into Dariel's side, nodding at the trousers he still wore. "He'll be ready soon."

Dariel bobbed his head, disappointed but understanding. He stood up and began to unbutton his trousers.

"Wait!" Athens held up a hand to him. "Slow down. You had your fun, that's hardly fair." He stood and prowled over to Dariel, who continued to step back as a tease until he hit the desk on the far wall and had no choice but to give in.

Athens pressed his frame against Dariel's, palming his cock beneath the trousers, the only remaining barrier between them.

"I thought about this years ago, can you believe that?" Athens whispered into Dariel's ear while his fingers pulled at the zip and Dariel shimmied his hips to allow the material to fall to a puddle at his feet, his underwear following immediately after.

"I used to touch myself thinking about you." Athens pushed Dariel back with a giddy mumble, Dariel's bare arse biting into the glossy wood behind them as he was bent backwards and Athens slid down his body like a predator and his prey, all the way down until his mouth found Dariel's hard cock and he took it inch by inch as if he'd already done it many times before.

They would have continued if it were not for the knock on the door.

Athens pulled back, saliva on his chin that he quickly wiped as he rose to full height. Dariel stood, mind whirring with the delirium of unfinished satisfaction.

'I believe that's the master of the house.'

Chapter Eleven

It took Dariel a moment or two to travel back to himself, feeling the warmth of Athens' mouth disappear as the other man pulled back. He had been embarrassingly close to finishing, blinking away stars. The knock almost *annoyed* him.

Athens walked over to the door, pale body lithe and angelic; fine, red-black hair flowing with the movement of his hips. Dariel watched as the taller man leaned his ear against the door, hand already reaching for the handle as he called out to the other side. "Godwin? Are you ready?" Athens looked up to where Dariel was still resting against the desk and winked. *Cruel.*

Dariel blinked as a response and stood up, suddenly very conscious of his nakedness, ready to pick up his discarded shirt.

A muffled sound came from behind the door. "I am, yes. I... would you both..." Godwin still sounded unsure of his words, nerves radiating even from the landing.

"How would you like us, Godwin?" Athens asked sincerely.

How would you like us served? Dariel held his shirt against his privates, hoping it would dull every overwhelming sensation coursing through his veins.

"There's some... behind you, to the right, in the wardrobe.

Inside there are two silk robes. Dressing gowns. If you wouldn't mind putting them on? I had to guess sizes but..."

Athens bit his lip and closed his eyes, suppressing *laughter?*

Dariel frowned, then his companion stared at him, face back to being serious.

'This man is too sweet.'

Dariel relaxed into a smile. Athens wasn't judging, he was holding back joy.

"Well then, we better do as the master of the house says," Dariel said, loud enough to be heard from beyond the door. He dropped his shirt and walked over to the other side of the room to trace his fingers over the mahogany wardrobe before pulling the pin that held the doors closed. Athens was by his side a second later, the taller man's presence gracing Dariel's back with the warmth of breath. Athens' hand wandered around to Dariel's cock, snaking around his length as Dariel reached up to pull out the silk shawls.

Dariel closed his eyes and melted into the touch, but the first moan of pleasure he let out shot his eyes wide open in realisation.

'We need to wait for him now. It's unfair we're leaving him out.'

'Oh, I know," Athens' grip loosened slightly. **'But I still want you now.'** He pleaded into their minds.

The two separated with mild difficulty and examined the gowns they'd been left with. The finest deep red silk embroidered with black lace with a sash of black and gold ribbon woven through the belt loops.

Athens held his robe up, eyes the size of golf balls as he examined the material. "Damn, this has my name written all over it. It's a dream." He scrunched the fabric between his long fingers, intensely analysing.

Dariel rested his flat on the bed. "It's a beautiful design," he said, dusting his fingers over the detailing within the lace. He then turned around to see the other man had already slipped his on, and was twirling around in it, hair blending into the colours almost *perfectly.* It truly was made for Athens; the vampire tying it loosely at the waist to still show off the triangle of chest in the middle. The silk hung off him as smoothly as flowing water.

Dariel quickly dressed himself in his own robe, wrapping the flaps of material around his body slightly tighter. It felt like heaven over his back and shoulders, truly one of the most divine things he'd ever allowed himself to wear.

"May I come in?" Godwin called out, and after absorbing each other's appearance, the pair of them strode back over to the door, approving Godwin's entrance.

The older looking man entered slowly, dressed in a robe not too dissimilar, though his was much less fancy. It was the deep green of a forest, but instead was trimmed in a simple strip of pale gold. No lace or extra detailing, though still of the finest silk.

He looked hesitant, chewing the inside of his cheek, causing his moustache to twitch. He smelled of pine, the fresh shower scent swirling into Dariel's nostrils.

Godwin closed the door behind him and stepped before the pair, hands grasped loosely in front of him.

"Oh," Godwin sighed with a smile, pulling at the chord around his waist, "you both look so handsome."

Dariel was still warm from his previous endeavour with Athens, but hearing Godwin's soothing voice again sent him spiralling. His breathing went entirely out of control as he eyed Godwin up and down. The other man's chest was slightly exposed, showing the bed of greying hair rising up his sternum, matching the coarse, pale hairs on his solid calves. Dariel gulped, fully hard.

There was a brief pause of *'what next?'* before anyone spoke again. Dariel was already imagining all the positions he hoped to give and experience over the course of the night, and tried to hold back the begging he was so close to doing.

Athens stepped forward, hands loose by his side. "You know the man I am, yes?" He took a sharp inhale and held on in anticipation of Godwin's response, standing eye level with the man in front of him.

Their host smiled, lowering his head. "Oh, yes. I do. I believe I figured it out a while ago. You are okay with... going ahead, yes?"

Athens breathed out. "Of course, it's nice not having to make a big deal of it."

"Well you are one of the most beautiful men I have ever encountered, dear Athens." He held Athens' shoulder and squeezed. "I'm very glad I found you. Glad it will be you." Mild melancholy laced his voice.

Dariel inwardly winced. *He still thinks he's going to die tonight.*

Athens just smiled.

"And Dariel," Godwin had a nervous cough, looking down slightly at Dariel's body, "have I, erm..." their host blushed, pulse quickening at his discovery, "or was that Athens' doing?"

The only thing Dariel could do was laugh, eyes closed to save embarrassment, until a warm, rough hand found the shape of his neck and entered his space. He reopened his eyes to meet the deep browns, greens and golds of Godwin's irises; thick, light brown eyebrows hanging over his brow in a permanent but soft scowl. His glasses had been removed, allowing Dariel to fully admire the beauty of the man's eyes. He gulped again. "Both," he panted out, maintaining focus as he stepped even closer so their bodies were almost touching. Godwin was a good few inches taller than Dariel, so he let his head press into Godwin's chest, focusing in on the strong beating of his heart.

A ghost of a hand reached for his erection, and he almost pushed fully into it. If it were not for the sudden hunger pangs he felt, causing him to push away abruptly in a panic.

He shouldn't feel hungry, but sometimes arousal clouded his senses. He couldn't think straight.

Godwin staggered back a little, fear in his eyes. "Oh, I'm sorry, was that too soon? Are you not... you don't have to..."

'You okay?'

'I'm fine, sorry, yes. He's... I need to fuck or be fucked in the next half hour, or I might scream.'

Athens answered for him, making a small noise from deep in his throat. "He's hungry. He'll be fine in a moment. You can have your fun with him soon."

Godwin's gaze settled. "And you?" he questioned innocently.

Athens raised his head but looked down slightly, walking over to Godwin and placing a finger under his chin, indicating he had maybe an inch or two on their host. "My body is yours tonight, dear Godwin. Do as you please," he promised in a sensual whisper.

Dariel watched Godwin's lips part slightly as Athens held him up, desire in both men's eyes.

"Shall we?" Letting go of Godwin and pacing backwards, Athens lifted an arm and pointed towards the bed as elegantly as the Creation of Adam, his long sleeve flowing alongside his hair in one fluid motion, like a fairy prince from a childhood tale.

If the vampires of fiction were truly real, Athens was the closest thing to a king to Dariel. A regal vampire lord who lived in the crumbling ruin of a castle in the deepest shadows in the corner of the world.

Maybe this could be their castle.

Godwin looked to be moving over to the bed, but he held back, turning to face Athens again. The way Athens looked down to Godwin then flicked his gaze over to Dariel almost sent him to his knees. It did not feel like only moments ago his tongue had been between Athens' legs, the man above him fully surrendering to the touch. No, now he believed he would need to win back that privilege again, as the taller man lifted his head high and held the room with a ten-foot presence.

Ruin me, Athens.

"Tell us how you hoped this evening would begin," Athens practically demanded; a lord to his subjects.

Dariel stayed silent, stepping over to stand side by side with Godwin, their arms brushing.

"The bed, please. I want you both lying on the bed. So I can take my time. So *we* can take our time."

Oh, this is going to be fun.

Dariel did not wait for Athens to move first, he already picked his side and lay himself down to the left of Godwin, making sure his robe covered everything. He was joined by Athens, who lay himself down to Godwin's right with far more artistic control. Their minds touched briefly as they both became offerings to the man who now stood at the foot of the bed, breathing heavily.

"Are you both okay with this?" Their host double checked, unsure in himself still.

"More than," Dariel said, tipping his head against the soft bedding. "I want you." He let it all out.

Athens grinned. "I'm waiting."

The base of the bed dipped as a third body joined them, Godwin kneeling between the pair of them, hands raising to undo each belt at the same time.

Athens sighed quietly in satisfaction.

The silk pooled to each side of their bodies as Godwin traced a calloused hand all the way up from their ankles to their bare torsos, taking his time stroking fingers over every curve, every angle, sending shivers down Dariel's spine. They had to share the experience; it was going to be exquisite.

'So rough and gentle at the same time.'

'He's done this before, surely, he—' Dariel was the first to make a sound, breath betraying him. If he locked eyes with Athens now, the other vampire would never let it down that he crumbled at the slightest touch, so instead he looked up to a kneeling Godwin, the other man's eyes flicking from both bodies before him rapidly, as if one may disappear any minute, though he didn't know which. His hand slowly raised up Dariel's body until it found his chest and it stilled, wide palm casing the dead heart beneath the ribs.

He trembled slightly, as if he were holding a fragile ornament, but the pressure grew more intense as confidence welled into him. He looked fascinated.

"It is true you possess no heart," he said to the both of them.

Dariel heard Athens shake his head against the sheets. "Not *no* heart. An un-beating one. Our hearts still fill the space, we are human after all. Like you said before, it still beats in our souls."

"That is true," Godwin said softly.

Dariel watched the rise and fall of Athens' chest where Godwin's other hand was pressed, glad in that moment his heart no longer beat, for it may have betrayed him entirely.

"Forgive me, it was only an observation. A confirmation of my findings." Godwin pulled back.

Athens adjusted himself to a seating position against the pillows, his body exposed as the silk slid beneath him. He lifted his knees slightly, parting his legs.

Hunger rose in Dariel's stomach again, throat parched.

Godwin's eyes fixed to Athens' body as he repositioned his own to sit back, knees and ankles clicking as he did so. The belt of his own shawl loosened to expose his chest almost entirely. Dariel stayed lying down, too loose to move as his eyes fixed between the pair of them, the dim yellow glow in the room illuminating them both like saints.

"What else did you wish to prove?" Athens asked lazily, desire coating his words.

"Most has been proven, including if it is possible for vampires to experience arousal." Godwin's hand wandered over to Dariel's left thigh, dangerously close to a movement that definitely would have taken Dariel over the edge. "I'm glad I learned that already."

Now both pairs of eyes burned into Dariel.

"He's a pretty one, isn't he?" Athens said.

"An angel," Godwin added.

'I'm holding on but I...'

'Don't, let go.'

Dariel caved, struggling to quickly drag himself up and remove the sleeves of the gown, baring his skin entirely to the two men before him. "Someone touch me, I can't take this."

Godwin moved first, grabbing Dariel's pulsing cock and rubbing slow and hard, thumb circling the tip. Athens moved to cover Dariel's body with his arms and sunk down into a kiss, stealing Dariel's breath.

The two men worked effortlessly to pleasure Dariel, allowing him to fully disappear into his own world of bliss. Godwin worked both his hands around Dariel's thighs and groin, pushing Dariel's legs up and apart further to work his fingers around sensitive parts, causing Dariel to shake as his body became completely undone. Athens worked his mouth over Dariel's lips, neck, and torso, leaving no area unexplored. Dariel raised his hips and back, whimpering and yearning to be touched and held deeper by both men. They had to practically pin him down as tension rose and Dariel grew close to release.

Athens pulled away and looked into Dariel's eyes briefly before turning his head to watch Godwin hard at work.

Dariel reached out to pull Athens' chin back towards him with grabbing hands. "Come back," he pleaded, almost silently with the remaining breath in his lungs, lips sore.

'I want to watch you come.' Athens laid his head on Dariel's chest, hands soft against his skin.

Dariel propped himself up as much as he could.

'You're so close.'

"Dariel," Godwin said low and gravelly, speeding up his fist, jerking Dariel to the rhythm of his own raging pulse.

"I... *ahh,*" Dariel flopped back into the pillows as he came, grasping tight to the sheets, blind and numb for the split second before he felt Athens' tongue on his stomach and Godwin's hands massaging his thighs.

'Oh, you taste divine.'

'I... huh...'

Godwin's mouth lowered onto Dariel's softening length, licking every inch clean.

"Beautiful," the human said once he swallowed, greedy eyes meeting Dariel's own.

"That didn't take long, did it?" Athens said in a teasing manner, prowling like a cat back up towards the side of Dariel's face, and planting a kiss onto his shoulder. His fingers twirled over his sternum as their bodies hugged flat beside each other.

'Kiss me, you're next.'

'You up for the challenge?'

Dariel *knew* Athens had slipped his own free fingers into himself, felt the rocking of hip bones against his side, but as Athens' lips touched his again, he drowned into them and forgot how to breathe.

Godwin rose up, moving around, and stroked a hand over Athens' shoulder to brush his hair back, then traced his hand down the shape of Athens' body until his fingers wove around and replaced Athens', the vampire instinctively turning onto his back to let Godwin have full access to him.

"Forgive me if I... Oh, Athens."

Dariel watched their host gently plunge his middle finger inside Athens, Godwin's brow clenched tight.

"I've never done this before, please stop me if it's not good," Godwin said softly, stroking Athens' hair away from his face. At that, Athens reached down to assist, directing Godwin towards his own wants and desires.

'What does he feel like?'

'Bliss.' Was all Athens responded with, head tipping back, mouth wide as Godwin worked his finger deeper, thumb and forefinger rubbing Athens' clit.

Athens gasped, moving his hands away as Godwin found his rhythm. Dariel instinctively reached out to hold the nearest palm to him as his other hand was occupied with his own pleasure.

He watched Athens reach up with his left hand to stroke the hair from Godwin's brow, sitting up a little and leaning closer.

Godwin pulled back, removing his fingers. "Sorry, I should say. I... I'm not comfortable with kissing. Well, to an extent. I'm just not, you know. It doesn't really do much for me. I can kiss you both if you'd like but..." his eyes flashed between them, hands loosely flopped, open palmed to his sides as if asking for forgiveness.

"No kissing then, we don't have to," Athens said, looking to Dariel to agree, legs still wide apart.

"I don't care what we do, whatever feels right to you, sweetheart," Dariel added, reaching over to squeeze Godwin's arm.

Godwin nodded slightly. He didn't seem fully convinced.

"I'm sorry, I ruined the moment didn't I?" His face winced in shame.

"Not at all," Athens promised, rubbing himself slowly. Godwin's eyes then wandered back to the body before him.

"It would have ruined the moment if you started doing things you weren't comfortable with, we would have very quickly been able to tell," Dariel reassured the man to his side, still holding Athens' free hand. "What do you want to do?" He stared intently at their host.

"Can one of you..." Godwin looked down at himself, thick cock now in hand. Dariel's eyes widened.

"Oh my pleasure! Only right I return the favour." Dariel winked and crawled over, spreading Godwin's thighs apart.

It had been a long time since he'd had a man inside his mouth, and yet now he'd had two in one night, so close together. He remembered the taste of Athens as he eased his mouth up and down Godwin's length, the new flavours warming his taste buds; Godwin crying out.

Athens wasted no time in joining in, wrapping his arms around Dariel's waist behind him, and squeezing his hands around

Dariel's filling girth. If his mouth wasn't occupied, he would have screamed.

Godwin held tightly onto Dariel's hair, Athens on Dariel's back as the three of them moved together as one.

'I never want this to stop.'

'It doesn't have to.'

'We're still sticking to the plan, yeah? He's not... we're not leaving him.'

'Of course, none of us are going anywhere any time soon.'

'He tastes...'

'Better than me?'

'Different. But I'd have to taste you again to be sure.'

'Whatever you say, darling.' Athens quickened his hand actions, cupping and squeezing Dariel's balls at the same time; the slender, tattooed arm keeping him locked tightly in place.

Dariel struggled to swallow, nearly gagging—he was out of practice.

'Touch yourself.'

'Demanding again, are we?'

'I want to feel your hand against my back.'

A few minutes passed before Godwin cried out, nearly pulling Dariel's hair out and calling his name.

Godwin fell back as Dariel swallowed all he could, blinking deeply. As they parted, Athens lifted Dariel up and pulled his body flush against his chest, leaning back to sit against the pillows so both their legs could stretch out, and Dariel was sat on top of him. Then Athens inserted a finger into Dariel's mouth, coaxing ragged breaths as he grasped their free hands together and slid Dariel's fingers between both their legs, forcing Dariel to tease Athens' entrance.

Dariel arched at the restraint, moaning out, Athens not letting go.

'Deeper, you can't hurt me.' Athens shuffled them back slightly to let Dariel bend forwards to work his fingers in more.

'I... I...'

'Aww, you can't even think straight.'

"Gentlemen," Godwin said, breathing and pulse slowing back to a normal rate.

"Yes, dear?" Athens said completely settled and sure, despite Dariel squirming on top of him, stroking himself in one hand as he fluttered his fingers between Athens' folds.

"I can't stop looking at you both. You're beautiful. Angels sent from heaven. Just for me."

"Just for you, Godwin. Now touch yourself when you address us, it's bad form not to," Athens insisted.

Godwin nodded frantically as Dariel slowed his own hand to match the pace of the man before him.

For a minute there was silence, only heavy breaths and jerking movements, Athens' fingers slipping down Dariel's throat, pulling him back once more as Dariel came again, making a mess on his stomach and the sheets around them.

Godwin's eyes widened at the scene, rubbing himself harder in adoration of the art in front of him.

"Messy little man, aren't you?" Athens whispered into Dariel's ear before nibbling the tip of it.

"I need to be inside you. Need to feel you come around me."

"Challenge accepted. But let him touch you again, I love watching you both react to each other." Athens said it loud enough for Godwin to hear. A bleeding ink smile spread across their host's face.

"Come here now, Dariel," Godwin demanded as Athens released him.

Dariel raised to his knees and shuffled towards Godwin before sitting up and resting both hands on his shoulders. "Is that how you talk to your elders?"

Godwin's mouth fell open, desire the only thing shining in his eyes. Dariel swallowed at the same time the human did, both their throats bobbing in sync. "How did you imagine touching me?"

In response, Godwin eased himself back off the bed and wandered over to the bedside drawer, pulling out a box of condoms and a bottle of lube.

Athens made a giddy sound, still lying relaxed on the bed, fingers mindlessly circling through the hairs between his legs.

'He's gonna fuck you silly.'

'God, you make it sound so...'

'And I get to watch.'

"Can you... erm, get into position?" Godwin was back to nerves again, despite what they'd all just done together.

Athens raised a brow and turned to face Dariel on the bed. **'Go on then, do as the master says.'** He parted his legs to tease, a sheen coating the entire length of his lips.

Dariel got himself onto all fours, eyes focused solely on the feast at the head of the bed as Godwin stepped back around the back of the bed and squirted lube onto his fingers.

"Tell me if I hurt you," Godwin said gently, cold hands parting Dariel's cheeks slightly before inserting his first finger.

At the slight pain, Dariel winced and bent his elbows more, but he tried to remain focused on Athens in front of him, still teasing his own fingers between his legs, other hand tracing lines across his soft chest.

Godwin found his rhythm, pushing the finger deeper and deeper, Dariel moaning their names over and over as he was rocked into the mattress and even Athens started crying out in glee.

Godwin eventually decided to try two fingers as Dariel loosened up, but by that point, all Dariel could see was stars behind his eyes.

"Oh God... At least put three... *ahh.*" Dariel shuddered as Godwin pinched all four fingers together and coaxed them inside.

'That's it. Scream his name if you have to. You're coming undone.'

Dariel didn't even have the strength to respond, his thighs trembling.

"I can't hear you," Godwin teased as Dariel collapsed into the bed, panting for breath.

"Godwin. That was…" he tried. Knowing all eyes were on him. "I…huh. God."

"I think he's done for," Athens joked, eyeing Dariel's collapsed form, fists clenched into the sheets. "My turn."

'Fuck me first.'

'Rest a bit, Dariel, you're on the verge of passing out.'

'I'm not. I can go on. I…'

Athens rolled his eyes and sat up, Dariel not having the muscle strength to even move an inch, body exhausted.

He heard the movements as Godwin and Athens joined together, listened to them moan and gasp and chant each other's names as he came back into himself. When he finally managed to turn, he glimpsed Godwin's hands splayed out under Athens' neck and chest as he thrust inside the vampire from behind; Athens' teeth visible, hair tattered around him.

Dariel shuffled back into a seating position, spectating, and ignoring the slight soreness as he watched how they both went from standing, to Athens bending forward and Godwin arching down onto him, passion burning in their eyes.

'God, he knows what he's doing.'

'He was made for us.'

Athens looked up through his lashes, both hands forming fists on the duvet, his raven hair spilling over and pooling around him. It wasn't the brightest light, but Dariel thought perhaps he could see lighter roots on Athens' scalp. It was hard to believe the jet blackness of his hair was natural, but it made Dariel smile.

"You're not pulling out until you come inside me." Athens strained his neck around to instruct Godwin, which Dariel found ungodly attractive. He couldn't stop staring. Admiring. The fluttering in his lungs returned as he watched them both move faster and sharper, until Godwin finished and collapsed on top of Athens, forcing the pair of them into the mattress.

The three of them lay alongside each other for a while, recovering. Athens remained on his front, Godwin in the middle.

"I never thought I'd be able to experience something like this again," Godwin finally spoke, staring up at the ceiling, his broad shoulders pressing into Dariel's.

"It's been a while for me too," Dariel said, trying to follow Godwin's line of sight, analysing the patterns in the canopy of the cover atop the four-poster bed.

"Is it selfish?"

"What? Sex?"

"All of this. What I want."

Dariel shook his head and reached for Godwin's hand, clasping it tight. "Never. Never be ashamed of your desires."

Do you still want to die? The unspoken question.

A mild snore sound came from Athens' side and the pair of them turned.

"He's gone to the world," Dariel said, peering over Godwin's side at the peaceful form of Athens, tattooed arm up beside his face as support, eyelids fluttering with long black lashes shadowing over.

"He's like a sleeping fairy prince, don't you think? Like the ones our parents read to us as children," Godwin observed, lowering his voice.

"Did your parents read to you a lot?" Was the question that came out of Dariel's mouth, not: *I thought the same. Our sleeping prince.*

Godwin settled onto his back again with a low sigh. The broader man's body covering the sight of Athens on his other side. Dariel tucked himself closer into Godwin's side, lifting his knees up slightly. *For warmth.*

"My mother did, when I was very young, then it became the nanny's job, then as soon as I could read myself, it became my job."

Dariel stayed silent, dragging his teeth over his lips, deep in thought.

"You miss it, don't you? Being alive?" Godwin asked.

"A bit, but I am still alive, just not quite in the same way. Life is worth living, no matter how hard it seems. I suppose I am fortunate I get to live it forever, despite the sadness immortality brings." Dariel tried not to disappear too deeply inside himself with his response, mind gently teasing him with images of Annette, and of who he imagined Sparrow would have grown up to be.

"I am sorry about your wife. I truly am," Godwin said, eyes fixed straight ahead.

Did I make it that obvious?

But no shadows came this time.

"Thank you," Dariel said softly. "I'm sorry about your life too. I wish I could have been here sooner." He really meant it.

Godwin only nodded.

Less than five minutes had gone by before Athens stirred back awake and jolted upright, hair flopped all over his face and shoulders.

"The prince awakes," Godwin said, his voice merrier than it had been moments before. Dariel sat up too.

Athens formed an 'oh' sound with his mouth then blinked a few times, squinting to make out the room.

"Back from the land of nod?" Dariel jested, sitting up fully; ignoring the ache.

Athens took in a deep breath before rubbing his temple, looking away slightly. "I didn't fall asleep during sex, did I?" he muttered to no one in particular.

At that, Godwin grumbled a low laugh, wheezing as he did so.

"No, you were perfectly awake for that. Perhaps I worked you too hard?"

That was enough for Athens to snap his attention back to them both. "Oh, God, no. We were just getting started, weren't we?"

'I still need you inside me.'

'You bounced back fast, didn't you? We can wait, you know. After all, as you said, we're not going anywhere.'

Athens smirked but held off from making eye contact with Dariel.

"I'm not ready to end the night yet, I still haven't had the privilege of seeing Dariel here fuck *you.*" Athens reached out his tattooed arm to cup Godwin's bearded chin. "I can be quite stubborn if I don't get my own way." He pinched Godwin's skin, then sat up from the bed, shaking his hair out and looking back to the men on the bed.

"Where do you want me?" Dariel whispered into Godwin's ear, rubbing a hand down his side, and brushing through the thick hairs on Godwin's arm.

Athens moved around the bed to hand Dariel a condom and lube, stroking his shoulder and letting his hair tickle his side. "Give him a good time, then it's my turn."

'You enjoy drawing things out, don't you?'

'It's a special kind of torture. I can wait. He's going to ask me to drain him soon.'

'Which you're not going to do.'

'I'll have a little taste, nothing more.'

'Then?'

'Then you're going to be beneath and inside me all at once.'

Dariel closed his eyes and attempted to swallow the lump in his throat, turning back to Godwin. "Do you want it here?" He teased a single finger around the perimeter of Godwin's hole.

The larger man gasped and clenched his cheeks tight.

"You'll have to relax now. Can you do that for me, sweetheart?"

Godwin nodded. "Do it, I need you."

Dariel rolled on the condom, lubed his fingers up, and worked himself inside, a finger at a time. Athens remained behind him before slowly circling the bed like a lion, eyes fixed on his food.

Eventually Godwin relaxed enough for Dariel to insert himself, and the pair began rocking together, slowly, in long and drawn-out motions.

Athens mounted the bed again and lay himself down to face Godwin, hand ghosting over the dips and rises of the side of Godwin's body. Dariel slipped in and out behind, trying and failing to control his breathing again. There was no intenseness this time though, just slow, fluid movements. Godwin gasped with pleasure, and Dariel focused on how Athens stroked the greying hair from Godwin's temples.

"You're so good," Dariel managed to say, reaching an arm around to feel Godwin's heart beat out of his chest.

"Don't... stop," Godwin panted, rocking his hips back harder against Dariel's, causing Dariel to cling on tighter through fear of losing himself to the feeling again. He needed to stay present, he knew what was about to happen.

"Drink from me, Athens. I'm ready," Godwin said mildly.

There we go. This is it.

'Don't hurt him.'

'You know I won't.'

Godwin was terrified, his pace slowing slightly as his brain inevitably homed in to what he'd asked for, heart rapid.

'Stop before he...'

"Don't stop, please," Godwin begged, pushing into Dariel's chest then directing Athens as he said: "I'm ready now, I am. It's time."

There was a moment where you could have heard a pin drop, then Dariel heard a sharp intake of breath as Athens forced his teeth into Godwin's neck and the man against him tensed momentarily before relaxing again as his mind numbed.

Dariel still held Godwin's heart as it reached its limit.

Athens sunk down harder, feeding deeper from the artery.

"Beautiful." Dariel thought he heard Godwin stutter.

It was impossible for Dariel to hold down his own hunger much longer, becoming aware of every vein and artery inside Godwin's body as he slipped himself out and thrust in one last time before biting down into the side of Godwin's shoulder.

'We can't make a habit of this.'

'We won't.'

They fed in sensual bliss. Entwining their fingers under Godwin's right arm as the man between them shuddered and allowed every muscle in his body to relax.

'So sweet.'

'We should stop soon.'

'He tastes so much better than I expected.'

'Athens... we need to...'

Neither of them stopped, Godwin's heart fluttering and slowing a little as they began to let their hunger fully take them over, his blood sliding down their throats, warming their bellies.

"WAIT!" It was Godwin, jerking strong enough to knock Dariel's mouth away. Athens followed suit, pulling back, eyes a carmine red with blood smothered over his lips.

Godwin held his hands up in surrender, then pushed himself up to a sitting position. Dariel shook his head a few times, trying to return to normal. The remnants of blood coating his own lips.

"Please. I... I don't want it... not yet."

Dariel couldn't find the words, but as a bright red smile widened on Athens' face, it all fell into place.

This was his plan all along.

"I know you don't want it," Athens said, wiping his mouth with the back of his hand, painting the rose on his wrist.

You took enough to make him want to stop. Let him make the decision, Dariel thought.

"What?" Godwin sounded delirious, which made sense, they'd taken quite a bit from him.

"You don't want to die, you never did. We were never going to..." Athens reassured the human.

"You weren't?" Godwin's eyelids rippled, sleep threatening to take over.

"Not after knowing you for more than thirty seconds. We could never do that."

"But my memories... I..."

"Your memories are your memories. We're not touching your mind," Dariel added.

Godwin sunk back, flopping his head to the side in exhaustion. "Oh... oh." He closed his eyes, his heartbeat steady.

Athens looked to Dariel briefly before they both turned their full attention to Godwin.

"You should probably rest now, darling, we'll be here in the morning." Athens stroked Godwin's forehead, pressing his fingers to his brow, and allowing the man to drift off soundlessly, covering him in his green robe.

"Will he be okay? We drank a lot."

"He's fine, we'll keep checking in. He'll be out for a good few hours though."

"I thought we were going to kill him... accidentally."

"We wouldn't have," Athens said softly, standing and retrieving his robe from the floor. "He's just as stubborn as me, like I said. Too stubborn to die."

Dariel winced then stood, reaching for his own gown, and trying to calm his mind. "So what now?"

"We freshen up. Let's get that makeup off you." Athens walked around the bed to meet Dariel and take his hands. "Plus, I believe I'm still owed something."

Dariel relaxed into a laugh, all tension evaporating.

"Oh, you know how to play this game, don't you?" He sucked in his lips.

"I do indeed." Athens winked.

The pair of them turned back to the sleeping man one last time before heading for the door, turning the lights off. "You promise he'll be okay?" Dariel asked.

"I promise. We'll be there when he wakes up, he'll need some aftercare."

Chapter Twelve

Dariel followed Athens down the hallway to the room they now knew to be the bathroom, or at least one of them. The mirror was still slightly steamed up, damp on the tiles, and the faint smell of Godwin's body-wash hung in the mist.

"I can't wait to get to know him more," Athens said as he turned the shower handle, sounding as though he was referring to a new colleague, not someone who had passionately fucked him less than an hour ago.

"We know his body," Dariel half joked, arousal still lingering deep down as he caught a glimpse of Athens' flat chest under the gaping side of his gown. The bedroom had been dimly lit, but now he could make out every tone and shape of Athens' skin and body, and it was... perfect.

"Time to learn his mind," Athens said, testing the water, before letting his robe slip to the floor, baring his body again. No shame or shyness. The tattoo was even more intricately detailed in this new bright light, barely leaving any skin on his arm uncovered. Dariel wondered if Athens planned on getting more, perhaps the other arm or other parts of his body. He considered if he'd perhaps get a few himself, one day. Maybe they could go together. If that's what Athens would want. *Don't be silly, it's just sex, nothing more. Godwin made it clear he was never looking for romance.*

But what if Athens wants more?

Is that what you want, John?

"Stop gawking, you've seen it all now," Athens said, stepping gracefully into the shower and letting the water fall over his face.

Dariel didn't move, didn't know how to. *What next?*

'You could go and get our bags from downstairs. Maybe find us some towels? I didn't think that through, did I?'

So that's what Dariel did. He pattered down the grand staircase, the landing light reflecting off the large stained-glass window along the far wall to the stairs. He tried to keep his mind clear as he busied himself with the simple task. *Don't think about Athens that way. This isn't a romantic engagement. It was never meant to be.*

He dumped their bags in the spare room, and something flew past the window, dragging his gaze to the dark abyss before him. He took a moment to consider the view he'd have once the sun rose. How far he'd be able to see into the nearest town. He knew they were in the middle of nowhere, but only now did he truly realise *how* secluded they really were. He felt the draft emanating from the wooden gaps in the window and shivered.

He could hear the shower distantly and immediately went back to thinking of Athens. *Stop thinking about him that way.*

He couldn't. He wanted sex, of course, but with Athens... he craved something more. And he couldn't quite explain why. It had been forever since he'd opened up his heart to someone, let alone someone he'd only met hours ago. It was a dangerous move, but one he thought he could be strong enough to make.

He found a handful of neatly folded towels of various sizes in the built-in wardrobe to the side of the wall, almost too conveniently placed—as if he'd willed them into existence.

At least Athens had promised they could have some more time together, he would have to make the most of that. He closed his eyes and breathed in. *Enjoy it while it lasts.*

. . .

Before he went to join Athens, who was humming away to himself—tune carrying through the misty crack in the door— Dariel quickly slipped back over to the master bedroom, pressing an ear to the door to listen for life. Godwin was softly snoring on the other side, his pulse steady. Dariel sighed in relief, nodding to himself as reassurance. *Everything will be okay.*

He could go to sleep beside Godwin, be there when he wakes. They could talk, just talk. Godwin wouldn't start to fall for Dariel —sex was all they would share, and that was more than fine. Dariel would gladly enjoy their times in bed, but Athens was different, and he worried if he got too close to the other vampire, he would want too much.

This night was about Godwin though. About living. A fresh start, right? Whether Athens truly would reciprocate the yearning for romance Dariel had begun to feel or not, this night had meant the world to him.

So, whatever happened in the coming days, Dariel never wanted to forget this.

He crossed the hall as silently as a spirit haunting the walls of an empty castle, and slipped back into the bathroom.

Breathe John, I want you to live for me. You've waited too long.

'You took your time. I need you.'

Dariel instantly went back to feeling only pure desire, there was no use trying to suppress it. *'Now who's the desperate one?'* He slipped off his own robe, hanging it alongside the towels on the back of the door, blinded by the steam as he stepped in to join Athens, face cloth in hand.

The taller man turned to him and immediately pulled him close. A hug, nothing more, nothing less. Water poured into

Dariel's eyes, flattening his fringe to his forehead as he let his head tip against Athens' chest.

'You're very easy to want.' Athens rubbed Dariel's bare back, letting his hands glide over bones and skin, as gentle as a lover may touch. *A lover.*

Is that what you want, John?

Dariel raised his chin to finally glimpse into Athens' pale eyes; black makeup smudged down his cheeks. He smiled dimly at Athens' admission, raising the damp cloth to Athens' cheek to gently wipe away the darkness.

'Should I take that as a compliment?'

Athens' lip quirked as Dariel slowly removed his makeup. **'I gave it as one.'**

'And is this what you'd want?' Dariel's chest ached, brushing the cloth over Athens' now closed eyes.

'I would enjoy nothing more.'

Their connection was fragile. Something that could shatter any moment, so Dariel made sure he didn't break it. He leaned closer, lips inches away from the other man's, breathing up into his space as steam unfurled around them and water soaked their skin. "Your lips were made for me to kiss, I think." If he held it back any longer, *everything* would shatter, not only his metaphorical heart.

"Then kiss me. Kiss me, Dariel Hale." Athens' hands rose to hold both Dariel's shoulders, squeezing and pulling their bodies taut, connecting their lips as the hunger rose.

Dariel fell into it, fearing the end. *Take my breath. Take it all, Athens Daněk.*

Everything evaporated around them, the kisses deepening and lengthening, tongues exploring as they grasped at each other, never letting go.

'I want you.'

'I am easy to want.'

'No.' Athens broke the kiss, still holding onto Dariel; eyes wide. "No, I *need* you. Now. Now..." Their lips collided again.

'Then have me.'

Dariel leaned forward into Athens' arms, letting himself be held up as they drowned in each other. He could fall—could fall forever, but maybe Athens would catch him.

They kissed for eternity, yet not enough. Dariel's hunger grew and grew until he could breathe no more. He pushed up and locked their eyes again.

"Let me appreciate you." He panted the words with the same desperation of a man believing they would be his last.

Athens breathed in, dropping his arms to his side in surrender. He nodded.

Dariel took his time, kissing over Athens' shoulders and his bared throat, biting down softly on his Adam's apple. A cry of pleasure escaped Athens, music to Dariel's ears.

He worked his lips lower, wiping the cloth over Athens' hand-crafted body. *The gods took extra time when they carved him*, Dariel thought. He brushed the small towel over Athens' chest then around to his back, breaking the kisses to stare back into pearl eyes.

Once his lips lowered to the slick between Athens' legs, he closed his eyes, exploring with mouth alone.

'Oh, Dariel.' "Oh... Oh god..." Athens shook, hands grasping for purchase into Dariel's hair.

'I worship you.'

'You shouldn't say things you don't mean.'

Dariel stopped, still on his knees, looking up to his saviour. "I mean it." His lips stung.

Athens' chest rose and fell as his face dropped. "You really do?"

Dariel nodded frantically. "I don't enjoy lying."

"Then worship me, I welcome you, Dariel. Show me your devotion."

Dariel found his place again, tongue burying as deep as it could inside Athens.

"I could get used to seeing you like this." Athens managed to say after a minute or so, tilting his hips as far forward as possible without falling.

'Come for me.'

'Harder.'

Dariel obeyed, sensing Athens' reaction as he did as he was told. He buried his fingers into the fat of Athens' thighs, enough to bruise, then Athens' legs faltered.

"I don't think I can..." Athens cried out, finally lowering himself to the base of the tub. Dariel used all his remaining strength to hold Athens up as they slipped into a sit in front of each other, a tangle of limbs. It wasn't a large bath, but they made it work.

"I didn't get to finish you," Dariel said, sliding his bent legs to Athens' side, the cold hitting him as he was pushed out of the waterfall.

"I am quite a challenge." Athens smirked, breathing heavily, arms grasped to either side of the tub, his bone straight hair glued down to his skin, almost trailing to the bottom of the bath between his bent legs. "Come here." He leaned forward, cloth in hand.

How can he move on like that?

Athens raised his hand to Dariel's eyes and began to wipe away the mascara and stains of the night. Dariel let him, baring his face.

Athens' touch was gentle, as it always had been, and he worked on Dariel's face before he finished off on his own, stopping with the cloth pressed over the centre of Dariel's chest. They stared at each other in silence, eyes exploring faces as if for the first time. Their skin had been wiped clean—their final barriers dismantled.

"You're stunning. You..." Dariel's breath caught, words failing him.

Athens smiled, tilting his head slightly. "You mean that?"

His words shot Dariel straight through the heart. "I told you, I don't enjoy lying, so why would I?"

"I've admired you since I first learned you existed. For years I've wished to meet you. Now I have, and you're too good to be true. How could I have been so lucky to have been brought to you?" Athens reached out a long arm to cup Dariel's cheek—Dariel melting into the touch, elbows on his knees and hands clasped in front of him.

"Godwin. He's the reason for everything," Dariel said, eyes closed for a moment.

"He brought us together. It's as though he knew we needed each other. The three of us. Right here and now. How could he be so wise?" Athens rubbed a thumb across Dariel's cheek. He was freezing now, but as if on cue, Athens pursed his lips then stood back up to turn the shower off. He held out a hand to help Dariel up. "Let's dry you off."

The taller man helped Dariel step out of the shower, and immediately wrapped him in the largest towel, ruffling his hair and waiting for Dariel to clutch the material around him so he could reach for his own.

"Thanks," Dariel beamed, shivering into the new warmth. The towel was soft against his skin as he patted his feet on the bathmat to warm up even more.

Athens didn't speak as he dried himself off, but his bright eyes said enough. He was glad for Dariel's company. Happy to be with him.

Dariel shook the damp out of his hair, drying his own body off and noting his own blurry outline in the condensation against the large mirror. *You're truly happy, John. I can sense it.*

"You look cosy," Athens eventually said, reaching out his tattooed arm to pinch Dariel's shoulder over the towel. Dariel watched the movement happen in the mirror, sharply turning at the sensation.

"That I am," he said calmly.

Athens closed the space, tying his own towel around his waist. "I think..." he started, gripping both Dariel's shoulders.

What? Dariel stared up, waiting for the end of the sentence.

Athens kissed him. Delicately, gently, with so much heart, and Dariel simply melted into the depths of oblivion.

'Bedroom?'

Dariel dropped his head as a grin widened across his face.

Make the most of this evening. Dariel nodded.

In seconds they were both stumbling, passion resurfacing as they scrambled from one room to the other, giddy, chasing the high of each other until they fell onto the bed, Athens pushing Dariel down firmly into the bedding.

They struggled to part as they edged further onto the bed and Athens climbed atop Dariel, shadow fully enveloping him. "Everything okay?"

Dariel let himself sink into the warmth of the other man's body. He wanted anything and everything all at once. He'd never experienced such intense desire for decades. Sure, it wasn't all about sex. He could go without it, he knew that, because to him, once a romantic relationship formed, it grew into a much more complicated connection. One requiring more than just the body.

But tonight, it would have to be only that. *That was all it was ever meant to be.*

"More than okay," Dariel said, shifting his hips.

Athens looked down, arms to either side of Dariel's head. "Finally," he said, bending his arms so their bodies pressed together. "Just where I wanted you."

And it was exactly where Dariel wanted to be.

"Anything you don't enjoy? Things you don't want to do or don't want me to do?" Athens asked openly, giving Dariel the freedom to be honest.

He couldn't think of anything he wouldn't want to do with Athens right now, so he said as such.

"Perfect." A quick kiss to the temple. "I'm going to sit on your face then, is that okay?"

Dariel almost laughed, everything was happening so fast, but oh, how he craved that. Already starving since the last time he tasted the man on top of him.

"Be my guest." Dariel readied himself, slightly adjusting his shoulders and letting his legs fully relax underneath the weight. *Have fun.*

Athens pressed down before repositioning his body to lower over Dariel's mouth, pulling on the reforming white curls atop Dariel's forehead that were soaking into the pillow.

"Squeeze my arm twice when you want me to stop," Athens said more softly as he began to move against Dariel's tongue. Dariel frantically nodded; hands gripped around Athens' thighs.

'Good. Like that. Just...like...' Athens let out a cry, gripping to the headboard above Dariel. They reacted together, Athens moving his hips slower as Dariel's tongue explored every inch of him until they moved in sync.

They worked until Dariel's jaw ached and he finally squeezed Athens' arm. The other man moved off him immediately to sit back into a straddle.

"Good?" Athens grinned, observing Dariel's lower body.

Dariel slowly licked his sore lips in response, slightly sitting up.

"I do usually enjoy... you know," Athens flicked his head, waiting for Dariel to understand as he gently rubbed himself down the length of Dariel's erection.

"Being in charge?" Dariel suggested, hoping he was right.

Athens reached a hand down to rub his clit, eyes locked to Dariel's. He bit his lip. "Will that be a problem?"

There were likely going to be more times with Godwin, but Dariel wondered how Athens would treat those times. If they'd have more time like this. *Could they be lovers?*

Thinking about it was going to ruin the moment though. So he kept on track. "I still haven't made you come."

Before he even finished his sentence, Athens laughed. "Oh, I know what will do the trick. I'll make it easy for you."

In the heat of the moment, he was prepping Dariel in hand,

drawing out more breathless, pleading, elated sounds from Dariel, then positioning the tip between his legs, teasing for a moment before slowly lowering himself down a little bit at a time.

They both gasped together as Athens squatted to his knees and rolled his body down to Dariel, bobbing up and down with careful precision, his burning desire plain to see.

"I was so close before, you can see how wet you've made me. Now finish the job, darling." Athens bent close to Dariel's ear with his final request. "There's a good boy."

Dariel tipped his sodden head back, arching up as pleasure rippled through him, Athens quickly finding their rhythm and lowering himself more each time until Dariel was fully inside him.

They wove their hands together like a final puzzle piece, calling out each other's names and speeding up until finally, Athens let go, shattering around Dariel's cock, his head tipped far back, teeth growing in.

'Oh, you have no idea how good that felt. Look how hungry you've made me now.'

'Bite me. Take it all.'

Without further persuasion, Athens' sharp teeth clamped down on the hollow of Dariel's neck and he *drank*, their bodies still connected.

'Consume me.'

Dariel wasn't sure whether a fellow vampire's blood would have the same strengthening effect as human or animal blood did, but the blissful numbness one felt as they were drank from could not compare to anything else, he believed. He would let Athens drain him dry, and it scared him how easily he'd given himself up.

When Athens pulled up for air, Dariel's own blood dripping from the other man's chin and onto his chest, Dariel could wait no longer. He reached up and pushed Athens down, his canines finding Athens' neck as he began to take his share.

'Oh, you menace.'

'I don't hear you asking me to stop.'

'Drink up, darling.'

Dariel took his time, feasting on the sweet tang of his bed partner. Athens writhed and wriggled beneath him, as he had done, and Dariel had to repress his smugness as he rose from his drink to see what his work had done to the other man. Athens' red tinged pupils were blown wide, canines still protruding from his gums as he gagged back his pleasure and grinned.

"You're exquisite, you know. You taste like gold," Dariel said, sliding his leg over from straddling Athens so they now sat facing each other.

"Copying my own words now, are we?" Athens cocked his head.

"Maybe, but..." Dariel reached over to grab Athens' shoulders, his thumbs stroking over his clavicles and over the now drying blood from his neck wound. "I mean it, you're everything I could..." he stopped himself, acknowledging the tension in his grip as their gazes locked.

Athens was unfazed, bending over into Dariel's space. "Speak your mind."

"I want to..." was all Dariel managed, arousal hitting again as he observed every tiny detail of Athens' body. He quickly grew hyper aware of his own ragged breathing preventing him from doing anything else other than leap back forward to lock their lips once more, blood and saliva merging as their arms wrapped around each other and they became one.

'Ruin me, Athens Daněk. Devour me whole if you must.'

'Do you say this to all your partners on the first night?'

'You know I don't.'

You're different, I know it. I... He hoped Athens didn't get that last signal. They rolled back, Dariel once again beneath Athens as they worshiped every ounce of skin on their bodies. It was too much and not enough. He was full and starving. Satisfied and begging. He'd never felt like this since...

Athens is different.

.   .   .

After an eternity, they collapsed side by side, bodies aflame. Athens curled up to Dariel's side, hand tracing up and down his chest. "Oh, I missed a bit," he said, before licking up the last drop of blood staining Dariel's skin. They'd fed once more from each other, trying new places and coaxing out all sorts of sounds from one another. They'd thankfully kept the mess to their own bodies though... mostly.

"I will never tire of this," Dariel tried, hoping Athens understood his meaning. He hoped after what they'd shared, Athens would maybe want the same. Godwin would join their souls, but Athens would be Dariel's air. He would find the words, one day, to truly express his desire.

They slept for a few hours, bodies close. The next thing Dariel was aware of was Athens bending over to kiss his shoulder before pushing himself up, turning to the side of the bed and showing off the dimples in his lower back, right where his hair ended. Dariel admired the way Athens' waist sloped into his hips; soft cheeks pressed into the sheets.

Do not be afraid to yearn to love again, John. It's time.

They washed again, and cleaned up the few visible blood stains they'd unavoidably made—joking about how they would be redecorating anyway.

"We're going to make this place a heaven," Athens said, sat at the base of the bed, scrunching his hair into the towel.

"No one would ever wish to live anywhere else," Dariel contributed.

"I can't wait to see his face when he wakes."

A pang of worry hit Dariel; what Godwin had asked for; what they'd done. "He'll be confused, but we must explain, make him understand," he said. *What if something went wrong? What then? What if we've left him alone too long?*

"He will understand. I promise. He'll be okay."

Dariel nodded. "We were destined to meet him. Meet each other. It can't be for nothing," he stated, though it was more as a reassurance to himself.

The pair dressed, Dariel making note of the way Athens moved as he pulled on a stylishly tattered, knitted dark grey jumper over a thin, black vest top, and slid on baggy, black cotton lounge trousers. Dariel only brought bed shorts, not quite having prepared himself for the evening they ended up having. He thought back to the night before as he stepped out of the taxi—the thoughts that plagued him then. It felt like a lifetime ago.

"Need to borrow a t-shirt?" Athens asked, clearly watching the cogs whir in Dariel's mind.

Before he had a chance to respond, an oversized white tee was thrown his way. "Don't worry about giving it back."

They headed back towards the main bedroom, the winter birds chirping outside with sunlight beginning to beam through every window along the landing. The dawn of a new day.

Dariel entered first, his fresh clothes cool against his skin still, waves reformed in his now dried hair.

Godwin was awake, propped up on pillows with a book on his lap. He'd been up and about, drawing open the curtains and dressing himself in soft pyjamas. Dariel held a breath as he stared at the scene, but at Godwin's solemn smile, he sighed.

"Good morning," Godwin said, flopping the paperback shut and wiping his eyes under his glasses.

Dariel's chest lurched. *He's okay.* "Good morning."

Athens appeared from behind and held Dariel's shoulder.

"Gentlemen," Godwin said, pushing himself back against the pillows slightly, placing the book on the bedside table. "Did you sleep well?" he asked, though Dariel knew that wasn't the main question he wanted to ask.

"Pleasantly." Athens pinched Dariel's ass. "You?"

There was a mild heat in the room, the unspoken question waiting in the shadows.

Then Godwin asked it. Inhaling; brows tight. "Why didn't you do as I asked?"

Before answering, the vampires went up to join him on the bed, Godwin moving to accommodate them both. Athens lay down in the middle, hand caressing Godwin's chest. "I like you too much to kill you, darling."

Darling. Memories of the night before, all the way up to a few hours ago washed over Dariel's brain in a tidal wave.

Godwin didn't let his seriousness fade. "Why did you really not do it?"

He doesn't remember.

Athens looked away from them both, hair flicking over the sheets. "You never wanted to die."

To this, Godwin didn't react, which said enough to Dariel. He agreed.

"What we did last night, everything—every moment... I thought I was ready. It was everything I'd hoped for and more but..."

"You didn't want it to end," Athens finished for him.

Godwin winced a smile for the briefest moment. "Perhaps not."

"Well it's always good when we're all in agreement, isn't it?" Athens looked back to their host. "And it doesn't have to end."

"But my memories, what you are..." Godwin startled forward. "I wish to keep them, please don't take them. I will never tell a soul."

Dariel sat upright at the base of the bed, eyes fixed to the other two men. "We're not leaving, and we'll stay for as long as you'd like. Nothing will happen to your memories."

"I don't understand, you're both so young looking and attractive, you have your whole lives ahead of you—infinite lives! Why would you waste your time with me, here? It makes no sense."

"Does it not? Or does it just not make sense to you? Because Dariel and I are very content with our decision," Athens promised, tone sharp.

Godwin still stared at them both in disbelief. "But I can't..." He shook his head. "I won't ever fall in love... not romantically."

"And?" Dariel cocked his head, Athens nodding slowly.

"I can never love you that way! You two deserve..."

"Did you not enjoy last night?" Athens stroked Godwin's arm again, long black nails raising goosebumps on the flesh.

"Oh, more than anything... it was... perfect." Godwin blushed, hand lifting to his neck where two puncture marks still remained, slightly crusted over.

There's another two on his back. My marks. Dariel thought to himself, looking down in polite embarrassment.

"Well then, you loved us in your way. There is nothing wrong with who you are. We don't expect anything you cannot give," Athens said.

"But... Why? I don't understand."

"I thought we discussed this last night, darling. You understood there was nothing wrong with you."

"Yes, but..."

Athens sat up, slamming an angry hand into the duvet. "But nothing! We made our decision. We want to stay with you. It's not because we feel sorry for you, because anyone with a soul would. It's because we want to keep you company. We want to stay with you. We want to get to know you more, and we hope you want to get to know us—not for the creatures we are, but the men we were and will be. We want to share our lives with you now, and we're not expecting romance, we're not expecting anything you do not want to give. We want you to talk to us whenever you want. To help you pick out a wardrobe, and redesign the walls to be whatever your heart desires. We're going to fix that bloody record player, and keep your hedges trimmed, and you're going to cook us your favourite meals, even if we can't eat a lot. This is your home, not your prison. We want to help you live."

The only thing keeping tears from Dariel's own eyes was seeing them glisten in Godwin's. The man was speechless. Practically gasping for air.

"What..." He choked up, words disappearing.

"Will you let us do that? Everything we did yesterday, we can do as your friends. No romantic strings, none of those feelings. Is that not what you want?" Dariel asked, rubbing Godwin's legs from under the covers.

Godwin nodded, sucking in the remnants of sadness that hadn't already streamed down his face. His mouth formed a thank you, though no sound came out. It was enough.

Athens slipped off the bed, standing and tying his hair up into a high ponytail, heading towards the door. He looked even more attractive with his hair pulled back from his face, Dariel thought.

"Right, I'm going to catch a rabbit or whatever you have roaming around in these woods," Athens announced, pointing to the window on the far wall where the leaves and vines practically covered it entirely. "Dariel will keep you company." He reached the door. "Oh, and since we're going to be sticking around for a while, Godwin, just letting you know, we try not to drink human blood if it can be helped, unless the person is willing." He winked towards the bed.

Godwin leaned forward in protest. "Last night, the bottle... it was my own..."

"Oh, I know that. The sweetest." Then he left.

"You're really staying?" Godwin asked Dariel as they both sat side by side.

Dariel let his head flop onto Godwin's shoulder. "For as long as you'll have us," he promised.

"You bit me too, didn't you? I felt it." Godwin rubbed at his other side where the wound would have been.

Dariel's brow scrunched in apology. "Did I hurt you?"

Godwin threw him a genuine grin. "Oh, no. It was quite the opposite."

"Was the rest good?"

They smiled into each other's eyes.

"You were the best, Dariel. Although I cannot shake the thought I didn't get to return the favour."

Dariel swallowed and let his eyes wander down Godwin's body, desire pooling in his crotch. "Would you like to?"

"Now?" Godwin's voice grew raspier; hungrier.

"If you want. Or we can wait. We can do it now *and* later if you really want. I don't have many plans for the rest of the day. Whatever you would like."

Godwin blushed and swallowed, reaching for Dariel's arm. "Can we... now?"

"You want that?" It was Dariel's turn to swallow hard.

"Very much so."

They were moving before Dariel could really process what they were doing, his body positioning itself like muscle memory—already knowing what to expect from his partner. The bedside drawer opened, and Godwin moved to position himself over Dariel, strong legs straddling him as Dariel assisted in removing his drawstring shorts.

It was much softer than anything they did the previous night—each finger stroke drawn out in the way of a carefully choreographed routine. They both understood this was never going to be the final time.

Then came the final act, Dariel biting down hard onto the pillow as Godwin inserted himself all the way, jolting their bodies together as gently as possible—Dariel noting how much time and care Godwin put into each thrust.

"Don't leave us," he found himself saying, letting his thoughts spill out between cries of pain and pleasure.

Dariel fell asleep not long after, flat on his front with his arms pillowing his cheek. Legs and arse pleasurably sore. He heard Godwin leave then come back with the fresh nature scent of his body-wash; felt the sunlight on his eyelids before he turned his head.

He vaguely remembered hearing the door open again and a mug being placed on the table beside him. He felt the weight of another step over him and settle between them. An arm covered his body and pulled him closer, but he was fast asleep again before he could note anything else.

Epilogue

Two weeks later

"We leave you alone for an hour. Honestly Dariel, what a mess." Athens appeared at the door, closely followed by a flustered Godwin, oil staining both their overalls—the pair of them having come back inside after spending the morning fixing up Godwin's 1989 BMW M3 he'd not used since the early nineties. It was going to take a lot of work, but Athens said he was up for the challenge, so that's what had occupied a lot of their time the past few days. Dariel didn't know a great deal about cars, nor did he particularly enjoy staring at their undersides, so he usually just stood and passed them things as they both talked near gibberish about gears and suspensions. That day, he'd decided to dye his hair.

"Look at poor Godwin's sink, will that come out?" Athens said in half jest, Godwin already butting in and saying it was fine. Godwin stepped over to wash his hands and smiled softly, looking up at the dark brown disaster all over Dariel's head and ears and... face. *How did I manage to get it on my chin?* He thought, catching an awkward glimpse at himself in the mirror.

"Is that your natural hair colour?" Godwin asked, looking for a towel to dry his hands.

Dariel scrunched his face. "Not really, I'm hoping it will fade to more of a coppery blond. It's meant to…" he held up the dye box with a smiling woman on the cover with a very different hair colour to what Dariel was currently sporting.

"I liked the icy blond," Athens stated from the doorway, arms folded. Dariel couldn't quite make out if that was meant to be as harsh as he'd taken it.

"It will fade," he said, quieter and more embarrassed.

Finally Athens' façade cracked. "You could have any hair or no hair at all and it wouldn't change my opinion of you."

"Oh," Dariel said in realisation, dropping his head and blushing. A drop of excess dye landed on the cream bath rug beneath his feet and he bent to stop it a second too late, mind not really engaged with his surroundings.

"Right, that's it, I'm grabbing a bin bag. Head over the sink, Dariel."

Dariel did as he was told, Athens leaving the room and Godwin squeezing his shoulders.

"You're very handsome, Athens thinks so too. He says it a lot," Godwin whispered, the pair of them locking eyes with their mirror selves. "You will suit this hair!"

You are very handsome, John.

Friday night became Dariel's turn to cook. Or at least it was heading that way. He didn't mind, just needed to refresh his memory on *most* meals. The most he'd ever cook for himself in the past was the occasional rare steak or maybe a burger if he was feeling extra low on energy.

Now he was serving up the finest spaghetti bolognaise north of Italy. *Well.*

"If it's shit, we can raid Godwin's wine cabinet to wash it down," he said, lighting the candles in the middle of the table, the two men already tucking in. Dariel and Athens had very small portions, eating more for politeness, but Dariel still tried. Godwin seemed to be enjoying his.

They talked, as they usually did. Athens had been drawing up some design plans the past few days and wanted to share his ideas.

Godwin cleared up, as per his role for the evening, then they retired to the library, falling into routine.

Godwin lit the fire. Athens sat down last. "Well, what a lovely evening. I'm getting rather used to this, aren't you?" He addressed them both, free hand patting Godwin's inner thigh. "I definitely think green. For the box room."

"I agree, though I may be biased." Godwin nodded.

"I'll be able to take the empty boxes down to the recycling unit tomorrow, they empty the bins every other Friday, right?" Dariel joined in, thinking about how much they'd managed to clear up in such a short space of time. They'd emptied most of the downstairs in the two weeks since they joined him; the whole place lighter and more... alive.

There were just a few more things they needed to clear out.

And it was as if Dariel and Athens thought it together, right then, in that moment.

The fire cracked. Athens tapped his foot. Dariel rubbed his hands against the chair.

"I think it's probably time I get this thing off my chest. Since we're all sticking together now, for however long we want. You all deserve to know the man you take to bed each night. I apologise it took this long for me to bring it up." Athens spoke first, taking a sip of wine.

Dariel knew immediately. Maybe it was time.

It is.

Athens placed his glass down. "I met my maker in the early nineties, not long after I started to medically transition. He found me, charmed me with his words and actions—making me believe he was the only one on planet earth who would truly understand me. Of course I know now it was all lies. I was in my mid-twenties, but still barely felt like a man, and hadn't even been my true self for long, not in society at least. He preyed upon that." Athens absently grimaced at the memory. "We dated for years. Everything felt right, and normal... until it wasn't. I'm not sure I noticed when things shifted, because I forced myself to believe it should have been obvious from the start, but it doesn't really matter, he was inside my head without me having any power to stop it." He looked away, distracted by the thoughts before turning his attention back to Dariel and Godwin.

"I should never have introduced him to Sophie. Should have never brought him to our home. I was with him for five years, and I never even guessed what sort of monster he was. And I'm not talking about being a vampire, no, he was rotten to the core. Foul, foul man. There's not really much else to it. He came to our home one night in a fit of rage, never explaining why, and attacked me all because I tried to calm him down. He threw me into the coffee table, knocking me almost unconscious. Then I watched, dizzied and in pain as he stabbed Sophie with our own kitchen knife," he pointed at his chest with a sharp nail three times. "She was pulling him away from *me*. Tried to stop him from hurting me, and all I could do was watch her eyes glaze over as she lay in a pool of her own blood—my hands too far to reach for her. He staggered back after that, humanity taking over or whatever, then he looked at me, knife still in hand. It would have been a lot easier if he'd let me go with her, but oh no, he wouldn't let his precious little boyfriend die, so naturally he turned me. I'm glad I at least fell unconscious quickly, I didn't put up a fight."

It was harrowing to picture, Dariel clutched his shirt tight in his fist. He wasn't the only one carrying the pain of death.

"I woke up alone in the field behind the apartment complex as the sun rose the next morning, the sound of sirens and paramedics waking me fully. He'd just left me. Turned me and left me. Got scared and ran off, probably. Ha. Well, there was only one thing I could do—I went to track him down."

"I hope you killed him." This was Godwin, fist almost crushing the stem of the wine glass in his hand.

Athens raised a brow in surprise. "Oh, I did. I watched the life leave his eyes. Made it slow and agonising. I bled his confession to me; what he'd done to me, why he killed Sophie. He begged me to spare him, promising he would change, claiming he never wanted me to leave his life. It changed nothing. He'd taken my best friend from me, who was to say he hadn't done it countless times before through countless lives? What would stop him from doing it again? So I slit his throat and held his head back as his life soaked the grass beneath us. Beautiful image, sorry if I put you off your wine, Godwin."

Godwin shook his head. "You did the right thing."

"Glad we're on the same page then, would have been terribly awkward if you were against a little murder."

"Self-defence." Godwin shrugged passively—something Dariel noted he'd started doing a lot as he grew more comfortable with their company—finding himself again. Dariel smiled, nodding.

"The fire. My wife and... my unborn child died in a fire," he said. It was only right he shared this properly now—it *felt* right. All attention turned to Dariel. "I got home from work to see our house fully ablaze. I ran inside, no care if it burned me, and I screamed her name. I cried out for Annette, and it's been so long now, I don't even remember if she ever called back. I told myself she did for a long time, to blame myself. To prove I could have saved her, that it wasn't too late. I know now there was truly nothing I could have done. I'll never know who saved me, my dreams show me faces, play out all the false memories I created, but it doesn't matter now. I'm here, I'm alive, and, well... life has to go on, doesn't it?"

"Life goes on..." Athens agreed.

"Oh, I'm so sorry. I understand it means nothing saying this, but I mean it... You're both here now. Strong and alive and *human* and... well, my life sounds rather simple in comparison, doesn't it? What a fool that makes me," Godwin said.

"It isn't a competition." Athens shook his head. "It doesn't matter what has happened in your life, how good or bad you might think it was... we all hold things differently, our experiences and emotions are just as valid, no matter what. What happened to Dariel and I, it was horrific, something no one should ever have to go through. You didn't experience that, but you lived through something different, and it sat with you all the same." Athens patted Godwin's leg. "Though there were some similarities, I'll never feel what Dariel felt, he'll never feel what *I* felt. Neither of us went through what you did, though we can all still empathise with each other, can still listen, and learn and... well now we can all grow from it. Together. Isn't that right, Dariel?"

Dariel emptied his lungs. "John. My name is John."

Both men looked at him, a million questions in their eyes, until there remained only one.

"I was born John Farlan in Sheffield 1942. Married Annette Everett in 1962. I'm sixty-four years old."

'Well hello, John. It's nice to finally meet you.' Athens smiled then he clapped his hands, sitting back. "Don't expect my birth name any time soon, that's well and truly dead and buried, along with my ability to die, it seems. Funny how life turns out."

Godwin was the first to laugh, before they all joined in.

"You wondered weeks ago if I'd ever had to remake myself. I said no, but that wasn't quite the full truth." Athens wove in a hint of seriousness as his laughter died down, addressing Dariel—*John*. "I did, choosing a new name, a new way to live. Becoming Athens was a rebirth, and whilst I always knew *who* I was, I was able to start again, entirely from scratch, as the man I am now."

'It's an honour to meet you, Athens.'

"To life! And living in this palace of a home with two

delightful men for company. Forever." Athens raised his glass, winking at them both.

"To life." They both joined in, clinking glasses.

The body of Dariel Hale, or what was officially confirmed as his body, washed up in the Thames a week later. (No living humans were harmed in the process, they promised Godwin.) The wildest thing about the story was the fact it was front page news. It wasn't hard to forge, Athens helped with the plan—immortal manipulation goes a long way. But everyone now knew he was dead, which was the main thing. Such a tragic affair. Alcohol, they said. Such a shame. A true talent, gone too soon.

"Oh *now* they want my jackets, look at the price of that," he said, reading the news from Godwin's computer.

In slightly quieter news, a small obituary appeared in the paper for a woman who never really existed. It should have been recorded a long time ago. Long awaited closure for the 1997 case.

Frost coated the lawn the first morning in February; winter birds in the sky. John found Athens at the front of the house, cross legged on the bench, nursing a cup of blood; his gaze distant.

At the sound of the crunching gravel, Athens turned his head to look at John, whatever he was thinking about fleeting away at the recognition of his company.

"Come sit," he welcomed John with a pat on the wooden seat beside him, stretching out his legs. John turned up his collar—Godwin's coat—and joined him, the wind twirling his now light brown hair.

"Thought I'd find you here," John said, fixing his eyes to where Athens had been staring moments ago.

Athens hummed to himself, taking a sip before offering the cup to John, who accepted. *Fox blood. Interesting.*

"Having second thoughts on staying?" John felt it important to ask, despite the humour in his tone. He would probably be asking Athens this for a while, as well as himself. The answer was yet to change though.

Athens laughed distantly, "I didn't really have a choice."

John understood the man a lot more now though, and he read between the lines, grinning. They could do whatever they wanted, and they both knew that. "One day we'll visit a vineyard, I think Godwin would enjoy that."

Athens dipped his head, chewing his mouth slightly. "He'd be in his element."

"Well, one day he'll get himself a passport, that might be the first step."

They both laughed an aged laugh, one of lifelong friendship, then silence fell. John cleared his throat and passed the mug back, offering his gloved hand out as well.

Athens looked puzzled for a brief second, then he took it, his face softening. "There's something you came here to ask, isn't there?"

John's lungs seized, eyes widening a tad. "Was it really that obvious?"

As a reply, Athens raised their clasped hands up in the air and John smiled.

Ask him, John. It's time.

John squeezed their hands then let go, dropping his arm to his side and looking up to the sky.

Go on.

"Do you want me to start?" Athens said, leaning forward to catch John's face.

Live, John, live.

"Godwin was never looking for romance." John got his words in first, not letting himself guess what Athens was about to say instead.

"Yes," Athens responded, matter-of-factly.

"And we agreed we didn't mind, we wanted him in whatever way he desired."

"Yes."

'I can't read you.'

'*Try.*'

John closed his eyes. "I tried to make myself believe that would be what I wanted too. And I *do* want that, I want to stay with him, to help him with the house and take him on trips, but with you, I..."

My beloved, it's time to let me go.

"I want you romantically too." It was Athens, taking the words right out of John's mouth.

"What?" John startled, breathless.

Athens only smiled with his eyes. "What? Was that not what you were going to say? It's what I was going to say. I want to be with Godwin sexually. I want to be with you sexually *and* romantically. I want to learn how to love you in all forms of the word." He spoke as if it had been obvious right from the start.

Has it always been obvious?

"Will he mind?" John finally said after he let out all the breath from his lungs, brows tight.

Athens stayed cheery. "I shouldn't think so, but all we need to do is talk to him. It's probably already obvious to him."

"You think?"

"I do. I really thought we'd already made that clear, to be honest." Athens downed the rest of the blood, wiping his mouth with his sleeve.

John leaned in to kiss him, lifting Athens' chin. The other man melted into the touch as their breaths mingled.

A bird flew close past their faces, distracting John, causing him to pull away, startled. He turned to follow the direction it flew, then he saw it. Perched on the rim of a plant pot in front of them, twisting its curious head at them. At John.

A sparrow.

Sparrow.

'Your shadows, I've not seen them in days.' Athens rubbed a comforting hand over John's thigh. Was he seeing what John was?

I know. He thought to himself. *Sparrow.*

Goodbye, John. My beloved husband. Live well.

The wind kissed his cheek as the front door creaked open.

"Athens, John, it's freezing, please come inside, breakfast will go cold!" Godwin appeared at the front door, wrapped in John's white-feather coat—clearly the closest thing he could find for warmth.

"Oh, you look beautiful darling. Really brings out the tones in your beard." Athens said sarcastically, John already on his feet.

"Eggs again?" John asked cheerfully.

"With a fresh loaf from the market."

"You went to the market?" Athens piped up, confused.

"John took me yesterday, you said you had something important to do."

Athens beamed as he stood to join them. "Ahh yes, that I did. Come on then, breakfast awaits."

Playlist

'José Tries to Leave' by BAMBARA
'Nites Like This' by Choir Boy
'The Thinner the Air' by Cocteau Twins
'Starting Over' by LSD and the Search for God
'Switch' by Siouxsie and the Banshees
'Skin' by Rae Morris
'Voyeur' by Baths
'てふてふ' by Plastic Tree
'I'm Your Man' by Mitski
'From The Edge Of The Deep Green Sea' by The Cure
'Night Vision' by Mareux
'Licking An Orchid' by Yves Tumor
'Comfort Me' by Witch Of The East
'Take My Hand' by Luke Taylor
'Limestone' by Kaur
'Science Beat' by Have A Nice Life
'Lethal' by Cloudeater
'The Distant Past' by Past Day
'Tavo akys' by Katarsis
'Tonight (demo)' by Amira Elfeky

Acknowledgments

A huge thank you to everyone who has supported me on my author journey, enabling me to get this far!

Drink Up, Darling was a story that came to me in flashes in a dream last year, and I remember waking up and thinking 'I need to tell this story immediately'—and thus the rest of the tale bloomed. It was a lot of fun to write.

Thank you to Syd, Elpida and Zoe for beta reading and giving me faith in this manuscript.

Thank you to Ashe for the phenomenal cover art. I cannot stop staring at it, your talent blows my mind.

To the authors who kindly offered to blurb this, it means the world to me!

And as always, thank you to Maia for being my sounding board and knowing every single detail about all my upcoming stories as I ramble away on a daily basis.

About the Author

Harvey Oliver Baxter is a queer author and illustrator from the North of England. They are the author of the *Fallen Thorns* duology, as well as its companion novella *Forever Red*.

instagram.com/lastvanillasmile
tiktok.com/@authorhobaxter